D0396459

Karthik Delivers

AMULET BOOKS · NEW YORK

Karthik Delivers

SHEELA CHARI

Cataloging-in-Publication Data has been applied for and may be obtained from the Library of Congress.

ISBN 978-1-4197-5522-4

Text © 2022 Sheela Chari
Music note art credit to: mhatzapa/Shutterstock.com
Bike art credit to: Miceking/Shutterstock.com
Book design by Deena Fleming and Chelsea Hunter

Printed and bound in U.S.A.
10 9 8 7 6 5 4 3 2 1

Amulet Books are available at special discounts when purchased in quantity for premiums and promotions as well as fundraising or educational use. Special editions can also be created to specification. For details, contact specialsales@abramsbooks.com or the address below.

ABRAMS The Art of Books
195 Broadway, New York, NY 10007
abramsbooks.com

For Mom and Dad

I'm good at remembering things: birthdays, driving directions, ice cream flavors, words to movies, the smell of shampoo, the scratchy grass I landed on when Jacob Donnell and Hoodie Menendez pulled down my pants in second grade.

When I first started working at the store this summer, Dad would write down everything for me. But now he just tells me the orders and I remember. That's because I keep lists in my head. Once it's on a list, it stays there.

This morning, Dad helps me load the groceries onto the back of the bike. First the ten-pound rice bag and the packages of multigrain flour. Then the light stuff like spicy chips and boxed frozen dinners.

"Watch the road, come back quickly," he says as I strap on my helmet. "And DON'T GET DISTRACTED."

Which is what he always says, so I run through Carmine's fifty flavors of ice cream in my head, a trick I've learned when I don't want to listen to him.

It's hot and humid outside, and I can hear the bike's gears grinding as I pedal down Comm Ave. Comm Ave runs through Allston all the way to Boston, and it's short for Commonwealth Avenue, but the only people who say the whole name are from out of town, like my aunt and uncle from San Diego.

♪

Carmine's Ice Cream Parlor is also on Comm Ave a few blocks from the store, and by the time I get there after my deliveries, I'm like the Niagara Falls of Perspiration. Miles is already in a booth with Binh, eating a double Sloopy-Goopy on a cone while Binh draws in his notebook.

Miles (*short, glasses, crossword*) sees me and says, "You look like you have a wedgie."

I'm about to glare, but actually . . . that bike is always giving me one.

A customer from our store is sitting in the booth behind my friends. She nods at me as I sit down, so I kind of nod back, too. I don't really know her, but I've talked to her a couple of times. I think she goes to BU, because she carries a backpack with the college logo on it. Once she made me list all the different kinds of pickles we carry in the store (seventeen, if anyone wants to know). For some reason, she got a kick out of that.

I slide in next to Binh (*clean fingernails, mechanical pencil*), who's drawing a delivery boy on a bicycle. Only he isn't delivering food: He's delivering brains-on-a-stick. Binh's idea of sci-fi.

"What did you get?" he asks me. He smooths his paper with two fingers. Binh moved here from Queens, and before that, he'd lived in Vietnam. His family, the Phams, owns the Saigon Rose on Harvard Ave.

"Caramel Swirl," I tell him.

"He always gets that," Miles says. "Even though he's memorized all the flavors."

I take a bite, letting the caramel melt slowly in my mouth. "I like Caramel Swirl," I say. What's wrong with that?

"You like a bowl, too," Binh observes. "More ice cream that way." That's what's nice about him. Binh always sees the good, even with a bowl of ice cream.

Miles grins. "Nah. He's worried he'll spill on himself if he eats a cone, and his dad will know he stopped for ice cream." Then there's Miles, who finds a rain cloud with every silver lining.

I watch Binh add shadows to the delivery boy. "Where did he get the brain?" I ask.

"This is an extra brain," Binh explains. "He is a space alien, in love with an Earth girl. He is giving the extra brain to her."

"Ew," Miles says.

Binh grins. "Love is strange." When he isn't out delivering food, Binh draws. I wish I could be like him, that I could be good at something. The only thing I can do is remember stuff, but what can you do with that? It's not like drawing or throwing a baseball.

"Do you really know all fifty flavors?" Binh asks me. "I want to hear them."

"Sure," I say. "Appalachian Apple, Ambrosia, Banana Creme, Caramel Swirl, Chocolate Banana . . ." I get to Death by Chocolate when Miles holds out his hand.

"Stop," he says. "Next he'll be telling us the periodic table."

Binh laughs. "That's really good, Karthik. Alphabetical order, too."

"Thanks," I say. "Now you know who to call if you're having an ice cream emergency."

I'm halfway through my bowl when my phone rings.

"You delivered Ms. Carmichael's groceries?" Dad asks.

"On my way," I lie. If I tell him I did it already, I'll have to go back to the store right away.

"Ask her if multigrain flour is okay. We were out of whole wheat."

I slurp quietly on my ice cream. "Yep."

After I hang up, Miles says, "What does he think you'll do? Run away with the groceries?"

I shrug. Miles thinks my dad calls too much. His parents never call him, even when he was locked out of his apartment for an hour by his brother, Spencer. Our families are different, but our summers are different, too. One day Miles and I were hanging out on BU Bridge counting out-of-town license plates, and the next day I'm hauling rice bags for my dad. I haven't told Miles why. I haven't told him the store is in trouble. It isn't the stuff you tell your best friend. I mean, we don't even talk about girls.

"No, Karthik is a very responsible delivery boy," Binh says, grinning.

"But why does he have to deliver groceries?" Miles persists. "It's not like you delivering takeout, Binh."

"It is done in New York City," Binh says. "I know. We used to live there. Customers, they like it. They think it is convenient."

Miles crunches on his cone. "I guess. But can't people just carry their groceries home? That's what we do. Seems like a lot of work for one person on a bike, if you ask me."

"It was either that, or studying cell mitosis," I say, which is partly true. My mom had a book all ready for me until Dad announced "the plan."

The door to Carmine's opens and in walks Jacob Donnell, Hoodie Menendez, Sara Rimsky, and Juhi Shah. I try not to stare as they go up to the counter. Jacob and Hoodie order first, while Juhi studies the ice cream under the glass. If she notices me, she doesn't act like it. The only time she talks to me is when she comes to the grocery store with her mom. "Hmm," she considers, flipping back her super-straight hair. "Chocolate Banana or Caramel Swirl?"

Jacob (*tall*, *Red Sox cap*) leans against the counter next to her, eating his Black Cherry ice cream. "I hate banana," he says. Which is probably the only thing he and I agree on.

In second grade, Jacob sat next to me at lunch and shared a bag of chips with me. In second grade, that meant you were friends. Then at recess, Jacob and Hoodie pulled down my pants in front of everyone. And okay, it was second grade, and Jacob did this to everyone. But he didn't make them think he was their friend first.

Miles O'Grady moved to Allston in third grade. Life got better after that. Miles knew everything about Boston history—like where all the major battles were fought, what kind of bayonets the colonialists used, what they ate, where they peed. It could have been totally boring, except Miles made history sound cool. At recess we would think up stories about Martians colonizing New England. By then, Jacob had gone from depantsing certain people (me) to beating them up. So Miles and I devised all these ways of walking home that involved NOT running into Jacob. Let's just say we got to know Allston really well.

"Dude," Miles says to me now, "your ice cream. It's dripping all over your shirt."

"Your father will find you out now," Binh says.

I look down and wipe the dribbles off with a napkin. "So what," I say. Meanwhile, I'm straining to hear Juhi. I don't know why I care what she orders.

My cell phone rings again. "Done," I say to my dad.

"Karthik, come quickly. And don't stop for ice cream," he adds.

I get up to throw away my cup. I think of what I should say to Juhi, like:

- Caramel Swirl is my favorite. (friendly)
- Did you know Carmine's has fifty flavors? (nerdy)
- Remember when we ate ice cream at my dad's store when we were little? (nostalgic)

But I know I won't say a word, because I'm used to being Invisible.

I'm at the trash can when Sara (*ponytail, stick-up-her-butt*) whines, "Hurry up, Juhi. We'll be late."

I wonder where they're going. Jacob and Hoodie are busy snarfing their ice cream cones while Sara hasn't ordered anything, so she's standing with her arms crossed like an uptight cop.

"Hey, we can go save seats," Jacob offers. "Hoodie and I'll meet you there."

"Yeah," Hoodie says.

"Thanks," Sara says. "That's super-nice."

"Sorry I'm so indecisive," Juhi says to Jacob.

He smiles at her. He was already tall, but this summer he's had a growth spurt and now he's a good three inches taller than everyone, which I hate.

"You should get Rocky Road, like me and Hoodie did," he says.

"Oh my god, you're right," she says, like he's cleared up some huge mystery for her.

"C'mon, let's go, man," says Hoodie.

At the door, Jacob and Hoodie see me.

I wonder if I should have hid behind the trash.

"It's Kar-dick," Jacob announces, with his same annoying smile.

Hoodie jabs him in the arm. "What do you call your car when it won't work?"

"What do you call someone who drives like crap?" Jacob answers, snickering.

I've heard these pathetic jokes before, but it never stops Jacob and Hoodie from telling them over and over. I see them laughing outside as they walk away with their ice cream cones.

"You're really taking forever, Jooze," Sara says meanwhile.

I wait at the trash can, wondering what Juhi will pick. Will she get Rocky Road like Jacob told her to, or something else? Really, I don't know why I care.

"It's sooooo hard choosing," Juhi says. "They have ten flavors of chocolate."

"Actually eleven," I say before I can stop myself.

From the booth, I see Miles groan.

Juhi turns to me, surprised. "No, ten," she says. She counts on her fingers. "Chocolate Chip, Peanut-Butter Chocolate, Chocolate Banana, Mint Chocolate, Strawberry Chocolate, Death by Chocolate, White Chocolate Supreme, Merry-Go-Chocolate, Mexican Chocolate, and Chocolate Surprise." She holds up ten fingers.

"You forgot Everything," I say.

"Darn. You're right." Then we both stare at each other.

The girl behind the counter starts laughing. "I guess we have some ice cream experts here."

Sara Rimsky is not amused. "Freaks," she says in her stick-up-her-butt way.

I don't care. Juhi settles on an Everything cone (ha!) and on her way out, she eyes me curiously as if she notices for the first time that I exist somewhere other than the grocery store.

Back at my booth, Miles gives me a look.

"What?" I ask. "She did forget Everything."

JUHI SHAH IN 7 PARTS

- Hair ends (line up)
- Butterfly buttons (first grade)
- Favorite candy: licorice
- Righto!
- Three shades of pink sweaters (fifth grade)
- Writes poems when she thinks no one is watching (English class)
- Good at remembering? (like me)

Chapter 2

After Carmine's, I bike back on Comm Ave and think more about Juhi. Either she's an ice cream expert or her brain works like mine and she has a good memory, too. Which means we might have something in common. Which means we might actually have something to talk about if I ever speak to her for more than thirty seconds.

When I get to the store, I load up more bags in my bicycle and head out again. My next delivery is Mrs. Rodrigues (*cheap, mangos, broken buzzer*), who lives off Comm Ave. As usual, her buzzer doesn't work, so I have to call on my cell phone.

She comes down and asks, "Did you remember the mangos?" She always has a question or thinks something is wrong with the order. It's never "Hi" or "thanks."

"Yep," I say.

Mrs. Rodrigues peers into the grocery bag doubtfully. "Really? I need them extra-ripe."

So I repeat her order without looking:

- 1 bunch of cilantro
- 2 tomatoes, ripe
- 1 jar of lime pickle
- 2 mangos, extra-ripe

"Fine." She pays me and reaches in her pocket for nickels and a dime. Her tips always suck.

On Brighton, I almost run over someone's toe on the sidewalk. "Watch where you're going," he yells at me. I keep going, because usually the people who yell at you are even worse when you stop.

I reach Mr. Jain's apartment (*dhoti, wrinkles, tea*), which is on the ground floor next to a futon shop.

"Karthik, my boy," he says.

"Hey, Mr. Jain. I brought your tea and your box of frozen samosas."

"Perfect, I couldn't live without those." He looks past me. "It's one hundred and one today."

"No, it's ninety-four," I say. "It's ninety-five tomorrow, and on Sunday, it might get as high as ninety-eight."

Mr. Jain smiles. "That's right. You have everything in your head." His hands shake as he readjusts the dhoti tied around his waist. "This is nothing like the weather in Rajasthan."

Whenever he starts talking about Rajasthan, or riding camels, or walking barefoot, or whatever, I know it will go on forever. "Gotta go, Mr. J!" I say quickly. "All these deliveries."

On Harvard Ave, a new restaurant has opened next to the Korean bakery, across the street from the Saigon Rose. I stop on my bike to look at the sign: House of Chaat. I'm surprised, because I go to Binh's restaurant all the time and I haven't noticed this place before. He hasn't mentioned it either. Inside there's a line all the way from the counter to the entrance. A girl comes out the door and a whiff of fried onions and masala hits my nose. She's carrying a takeout bag and holds the door for me.

"Are you going in?" she asks.

I shake my head even though for some reason my stomach growls.

I get back on my bike and continue, turning on Comm Ave then Chester, until I find #24, Apartment 2C. I haven't delivered to this address before. Someone named Shanthi. When I'm buzzed in and get to the door, I'm surprised to see it's the same girl with the BU backpack from Carmine's. She seems surprised to see me, too.

"Don't worry, I won't ask you about pickles," she says.

"Good. I'd have to charge extra," I say.

She laughs. "Come in. It's so hot outside."

I set down the grocery bag in front of her door. By now, my hair is stuck to my forehead in sweat. "Actually, I'm not supposed to," I say.

"Why not?" she asks. She has hazel eyes like my cousin Kitty, and they always make me think of a cat in disguise.

"My dad says unless I know a customer, I'm supposed to stay outside," I tell her.

"Oh. Then wait here." She disappears and comes back with a small bottle of water for me. She watches as I gulp it down. It feels good.

"You can't come in but it's okay to deliver groceries in this heat?" she asks.

Who knows what goes on in my dad's brain? So I go inside. Her apartment looks beat up but nice: a faded leather couch, an oriental rug with a few worn spots, and a piano pushed up against the wall. A piano in an apartment? I remember all the fights a couple years ago when my sister wanted a piano and my dad said no. He made a big point of the neighbors complaining about the noise, and Nitya bitterly disagreed, while I listened to them go back and forth. (Of course, no one asked, "Karthik, do *you* want to play the piano?") Eventually Nitya got a keyboard, which she hoarded in her room—*Karthik can't touch it, he'll br-eaaa-k it!!* Three years later, the keyboard is covered in dust. Nice.

"You play? No one minds?" I ask.

"Oh, this?" Shanthi sits down and plinks a few notes. "It came with the apartment, believe it or not. And sure, no one cares." She begins playing for real now.

I listen to her. "That's *West Side Story*, isn't it?"

Shanthi stops. She really does remind me of my cousin: a thinner, sharper version of Kitty, but with freckles across her nose. *Freckles, piano, sharp.* "You know it? The opening is fantastic. Like this part." She demonstrates. "And this part here! I love it! Though I'm sure I'm boring you."

Actually, she isn't. I like the way she can talk and play at the same time. I'm about to say something when my cell phone rings.

"Hey, Dad." I try to sound normal, and not like a little kid getting badgered by his dad. He wants to know if I've finished the deliveries and then gives me a list of stuff I need to bring to another customer after I come back. "Right," I say and repeat the order back to him.

After I get off the phone, Shanthi asks, "You need to write it down?" When I shake my head, she says, "Are you sure you won't forget?"

"100 Ashford Ave, 4B," I repeat. "Tamarind, mint chutney, three two-pound bags of moong dal, eight single packets of Insta Noodles, half pound of potatoes, and a bag of spicy hot mix."

"Wow." She smiles. "By the way, that was awesome at the ice cream shop. You and the girl."

"Thanks," I say. It's strange that I'm not the only one thinking about Juhi and the ice cream flavors.

Shanthi fingers the white keys. "I wish I had a good memory. I still can't believe you knew all those pickles varieties in your store without even looking."

"There were only seventeen."

"I can't even remember more than two or three. You're so lucky."

I'm not sure I'm that lucky. I think of all the things I remember, like Jacob pulling down my pants or my dad crying when he found out he'd lost his job in Albuquerque. There are some things better to forget, but I never do. "I don't try to remember. It just stays in my head."

"Do you see things in your mind like a photograph?"

"No. I don't have that kind of memory. I see everything as lists. I remember lists best."

She listens with interest. "If I had a better memory, I would have done drama. At least I'm doing the next best thing, which is writing plays."

I stare at her. "You write . . . plays?"

She might as well say she's a rock star. No one I know is writing anything. My sister wants to be a lawyer and my mom is always drilling med school into me. I bet my mom would be afraid of someone like Shanthi. Which is why I start to look at Shanthi with new respect. Strangely, I notice she's looking at me the same way, too. Or is she just wondering when I'll leave?

"You know," she says, "you have a good memory. And every time I see you, I can't help thinking how you're the right age, with the right build, and the right hair."

"Hair?" What is she talking about? Is Shanthi one of those creepy people who stalks children? She doesn't seem like the type. She comes up to my chin.

"Maybe this is strange," she says, "but how would you like to earn a little money? Twenty bucks."

I wait, wondering what she has in mind. I pick up a Rubik's Cube lying on the dining table.

"I bet you can solve that," she says.

"No. I'm not a genius or anything," I mumble, putting it back down.

"Right. Well, the person who wrote this music for *West Side Story*—*he* was genius. His name was Leonard Bernstein, and around your age he got his first piano. His Aunt Clara mailed it to him one day, and he went on to be a famous musician."

"Yeah?"

"Yeah. I'm writing a play about when Lenny gets his first piano. That's what everyone called him."

Lenny. That's the name of our car mechanic on Boston Post Road. It doesn't sound like a famous musician's name to me.

Shanthi shifts her weight on the bench so it creaks. "To graduate, we need to have our plays performed in front of an audience. We usually hire adult actors, but I wanted to write about Lenny when he was a kid. You would be perfect—your hair is just like his. And I bet you could learn the lines super-quick."

It's slowly dawning on me what Shanthi's getting at.

"You want me to be in your play?" My eyes narrow. "For twenty bucks?"

Shanthi looks sheepish. "Yeah, that doesn't sound like much. Sorry, I'm a grad student."

"I don't know," I say.

"Forget the twenty bucks. I'll find some way to really treat you. But that's not the point. The point is you get to do a whole play. And I'm sure my advisor will say it's okay since they won't have anyone else young enough to cast. So what do you think? Wouldn't it be cool if you played Lenny?"

If I had a clue what she's talking about.

"But I'm Indian," I say. "Isn't Lenny . . . not Indian?"

"So what? We're all human beings last time I checked." She watches me. "And it's more than just your hair. I need a genius type to play Lenny. Someone like you."

"Wait, what?" I'm so surprised my voice comes out a squeak. I think of Nitya, who's always calling me Dweeb. She'd piss her pants if she heard Shanthi now.

"Don't be so modest. Remember all those ice cream flavors?

Learning your lines will be a piece of cake. Easier than remembering merry-go-round-choco, or whatever."

I smile in spite of myself. "It's Merry-Go-Chocolate," I say.

"Oh my god, I rest my case."

She makes it sound so easy. But is it?

"Wouldn't I have to practice? I have to work in the store." I think of my dad freaking out if the play cuts into my work time. So far, he's plastered signs everywhere, talked it up with customers, and even made phone calls advertising the free deliveries. I don't think this Lenny guy was part of Dad's plans.

"Sure—look, we can work around your schedule," Shanthi says. "The performance is the first week of September. That's when I graduate."

The first week of September. That's also when ninth grade, not to mention high school, begins. Mom is already on me to "be ready," whatever that means. She isn't thrilled I'm working in the store. Her idea of summer vacation is studying DNA replication for laughs.

"It's no big deal if you don't want to do it." Shanthi smiles unsurely. "But it would be majorly awesome if you did."

I spend a moment taking it all in. I've never been in a play, but while she's talking, something goes off inside me like this *ping*. "All right," I say slowly. "I'll think about it."

"Great!" She seems happy enough.

My cell phone rings again. "What?" I say, annoyed. My dad tells me that Mrs. Rodrigues thinks the mangos I delivered are spoiled. She wants to return them. "But she wanted them extra-ripe!" I exclaim. "They were extra-ripe."

"She said they were spoiled," Dad says.

I sigh. "Fine."

After I hang up, Shanthi says, "My parents can be a pain, too. My mom especially."

"Yeah, well I bet she doesn't call you every five minutes."

She shrugs. "She doesn't call me at all."

"Really? Why not?"

"Oh," her voice fades away. "It's a long story." She hands me a book that's on top of the piano. "Here, read this and bring it back when you're done. Find out about Lenny for yourself."

"Are you sure? I don't want to lose it."

"I trust you. Anyway, I know where to find your dad, ha ha." At the door she says, "By the way, I'm Shanthi."

"I know," I say.

Freckles, piano, sharp. Writer.

"That's right, you know everything."

"No, it says it on your delivery form."

"Oh. What's your name?"

"Karthik."

"Oh yeah." Shanthi pauses.

I suddenly blush. I remember Jacob and Hoodie at Carmine's and how she must have heard everything they said about my name. I wish she hadn't. I wish they didn't exist. And I wonder what else

Shanthi's going to say to me about them, and how embarrassing it will be, but she just smiles.

"See you next time, Karthik," she says.

Outside, the sun feels like a furnace as I hear a flock of birds flying overhead. I think of all the things that have happened today: seeing Juhi at Carmine's, her noticing me for the first time, Shanthi calling me a genius. And now me maybe being in a play. It's been a pretty good morning, which is surprising. I look at the front of Shanthi's book. An old man is on the cover with his arms waving wildly, conducting an orchestra in the shadows. So this is Lenny Bernstein the genius. He looks like a mad scientist and a little bit like my grandfather in India.

I slip the book inside the bicycle crate, not realizing then that my life is about to change.

Chapter 3

My family talks about things by not talking about them.

At dinner, Mom asks, "So how was it at the store?"

Dad says, "Oh, the same."

I wait to see what else he'll say. Like Mrs. Rodrigues being annoying with the mangos. Or Aasif saying we have to stop ordering broken rice because no one is buying it. Or me having to throw away the tinda from the vegetable bin because it's going bad sitting there for two days. But Dad says nothing.

"Pavan called before you got home," Mom says. "He said you could still come in for an interview." Pavan is my dad's brother who works for a software company in Worcester.

"Wait, Dad's interviewing with Pavan Uncle?" Nitya speaks up. "Dad's quitting the store?"

"Of course not! We're trying out something with Karthu," Dad says.

"The miracle," Mom says. The way she says it, it doesn't sound like one. My mom has this way of saying one thing and meaning the opposite.

She doesn't think much of Dad's plan. I know because I overheard them talking in the kitchen the night after school got out.

"Why don't you ask your brother to help you get a job?" she'd begged. "How long can we do this? Look at this board." She was talking about the bulletin board next to the refrigerator where she pins up the monthly bills.

"But I can't go back," Dad had told her. He used to work in a software company, too, when we lived in Albuquerque. "Not yet. Give me until the end of summer. I have an idea."

That was when I heard his gory plan for how to save the store. Me.

"Deliveries?" my mom repeated, like it was some made-up word in an alien language. "Can Cutie even ride a bike?" I thought this was unfair. I'm not a complete disaster. Although my summer was shaping up to be one.

"We won't put a lot of money in," Dad said. "We can borrow Raj's old bike, stick to just a few blocks. Plus there will be all kinds of sales at the store. Incentives. You'll see."

The next day, he pulled me aside. "There's been a change in plans, Karthu. Times are tough—it's only getting worse, so we need to save as much as we can." That's when he told me I had to give up my whole summer to bag groceries and run errands on my cousin's hand-me-down bike.

"What about Aasif?" I asked. "What about Nitya?"

"He's an accountant, not a bag boy," Dad said. "And your sister has to study for the SAT."

And that was that. I was so mad I didn't talk to my dad for an entire weekend. Then before I knew it, I was in the store, packing mangos for Mrs. Rodrigues. Dad put a sign on the store counter: WE

DELIVER FOR FREE! and in smaller print, WITHIN A TWO-MILE RA-DIUS. Why? Because that's how far I could go on Raj's lousy Schwinn.

Nitya stabs at her plate now with her spoon. "If we're moving to Worcester, you better tell me," she says nervously. "Speech and Debate is counting on me. I'm going to be captain in the fall. Just so you know, the move would ruin my life. No pressure or anything."

Worcester! My stomach drops. I just talked to Juhi for real today. I don't want to move.

"I did lots of deliveries today," I say quickly.

"Of course, Cutie," Mom says. "Who wouldn't use free delivery in this heat?"

There it is again, her opposite voice. It's like when she puts too much chili powder in the food and pretends it isn't spicy. We all know the chili powder is in there.

She points to an article next to my plate. This one is on open-heart surgery.

"What do you think?" she asks me. "Neat with the bone glue, huh?"

Every few days, my mom will give me an article to read. She's been doing this for as long as I can remember. When I was little, I'd find them tucked under my pillow, or next to my bowl of cereal. I loved reading them. The articles were cut from the newspaper or from one of the magazines we got, like *Nature* or *Time*. They would be on fun stuff like beluga whales or King Tut's tomb. Then we'd quiz each other to see who could remember the most.

But lately, her articles are feeling like a chore. They're all about medical breakthroughs or doctors doing things that make me squirm.

Like this one on how surgeons use special adhesive to glue back the breastbone after cracking it open to get to the heart. Just the thought of that, of someone snapping your bones and cutting your heart, is enough to make me barf.

Mom tells me I should be a doctor so we can have one in the family. It's good for medical emergencies, she says. And second opinions. I guess that makes sense, and Nitya's already decided she wants to be a lawyer. Blood's gross, she says. How come she gets to say that and I have to read about coronary artery disease?

"What, no thoughts, Cutie?" Mom says. "Maybe the store is turning your brain to mush."

"No, it's not," I say, annoyed. For a moment I'd thought of telling her about Shanthi's play. But she'd probably say the play will turn my brain to mush, too. "Did you know Leonard Bernstein lived here in Allston?" I ask instead.

I stop myself from grinning. It's weird how good it feels to have a secret from her.

"Who's Leonard Bernstein?" my mom asks.

"Oh my God," Nitya says. "He wrote the music for *West Side Story*. Remember, you got the movie for my birthday."

"I feel pretty," Dad sings in his Indian accent, which makes Nitya and me laugh.

Mom smiles. "Oh, that. It used to come on the TV all the time."

"There's a girl writing a play about him," I say. "I met her at the store."

"The playwriting student," Dad says. "Shanthi."

"Playwriting," Mom says. "What kind of job will you do with that?"

"You get to write *plays*," Nitya says.

"But is that a job?"

"Of course it's a job. We need people to make music and art. It's called living in a society."

"People need money to pay the bills," Mom observes. "This recession isn't helping."

I sigh. At almost every meal, my mom needs to bring up the Financial Crisis. I guess she's nervous about the store and us, but all it does is piss off Nitya.

"Well it's not the Great Depression, hate to inform you," Nitya says flatly.

"So what, it's still bad," Mom says. "When I was a little girl, my appa was a rich jeweler."

"Not the big house, little house story," Nitya says.

"It was hard to have money and jewelry and a big house," Mom goes on, ignoring Nitya, "then all of a sudden to have nothing. We were broke. We had to leave our big house and rent a tiny flat on top of a tailor's shop. Same thing can happen now. The only people who are safe are like Pavan Uncle, who works in a big software company." She glances at Dad. If he hears her, he gives no indication and goes on chewing his food diligently.

Nitya stirs the sambar and rice on her plate. "How come we have to eat at home all the time? Why can't we go out for Korean or Thai?"

"I like Indian food," Mom says.

"There's that new Indian restaurant on Harvard Ave," Nitya says. "We could go there."

"You mean House of Chaat?" I ask. "There were lots of people when I went by."

"See?" Nitya says.

"I bet they use MSG," Mom says.

"And if we're eating at home," Nitya goes on, "we should be eating brown rice. Or quinoa. White rice is full of empty carbs." Ever since my sister became a teenager, all she talks about are empty calories and sugar spikes, and she basically never lets anyone eat in peace. It's like Nitya thinks if she ate brown rice, she'd suddenly grow tall and skinny and wear tight clothing. The only part she has going so far is the tight clothing. Once I made the mistake of sharing my list of words for her.

"What do you mean, you have a list?" she'd asked, her voice shrill. "Why, what are my words?"

I had quite a few, but I decided to just tell her the top three: *short legs*, *gravelly voice*, *hair*. When she heard them, she actually cried. I couldn't believe she took it so seriously. Luckily, I stopped short of telling her the real word on my list, which was *hairy*. Because, when you see her, think of a skunk dying and plopping on top of her head. But hairy is much worse than hair, and she might have killed me. At any rate, I knew then I was never going to share my words with anyone ever again.

"Our ancestors have been eating white rice for centuries," Dad says. "They did just fine."

"Yeah, they were just dropping dead by fifty," Nitya mutters.

"Thanks for that ray of sunshine," Mom says. "But listen, Baby, you're right. We don't want to be like our ancestors. We want to be better."

"Oh God," Nitya says. "I've heard this a million times."

"But you're not *listening*," Mom says. "Success is about knowing what you're good at and then going after it. Take Cutie. He can remember anything. He better not put that to waste."

"Great," Nitya says. "He's a brain surgeon and what am I? A sack of rice?"

"You're smart, too," Mom says. "But as they say, use it or lose it."

I eat my food slowly. Mom says we should do what we're good at. But what if it's something different from what she thinks it is? Will she still be happy?

MY FAMILY IN 4 PARTS

DAD

- Son of a rice farmer in India
- Works as a programmer in Albuquerque until he gets fired
- Moves with his family to Allston, MA
- Starts grocery store near his brother (who he hates but he'll never tell us)
- Works 7 days a week (what's a vacation?)

MOM

- Daughter of a rich jeweler in India who went broke
- Wanted to be a doctor but got married instead

- Thinks success = doctor or lawyer
- Clips out articles for her kids (mostly me)
- Calls them Baby and Cutie even if they die of embarrassment

NITYA

- 5 inches shorter than she wants to be
- 5 inches wider than she wants to be
- Studies 24/7
- Needs to get ahead but is a pain in the behind (ha ha, get it?)
- Wants to be a lawyer and prosecute our parents

ME

- Delivery boy
- Remembers 50 flavors of ice cream
- Might be in a play (maybe)
- Noticed by Juhi (maybe again)
- A genius!
- Wants to be . . . ???

Chapter 4

The next day, one of the refrigerators quits working. It starts with a pool of water on the floor. Dad keeps going up and down the aisle, talking to customers in his Grocery Voice. He's terrified of the refrigerator leaking, but he doesn't want anyone to know, so he talks and talks. After a while, I have to stop listening.

"What are you listening to?" Miles asks from his crossword. We're both at the counter and I have headphones on. Miles shows up at the store when he has nothing else to do and brings the crossword with him.

"Nothing," I say. "Some junk I borrowed from Nitya." I found her old iPod last night and it has the soundtrack to *West Side Story* on it, which I'm listening to on repeat. I've figured out the story just by hearing the songs. It's basically *Romeo and Juliet* with street gangs.

WEST SIDE STORY IN 5 PARTS

- The Jets are white, the Sharks are Puerto Rican.
- Tony, a Jet, falls in love with Maria, a Shark.
- The Sharks fight the Jets.
- A bunch of people die, including Tony.
- Maria (sad) wants to know, why can't we all get along?

As I'm listening to the music, Miles notices the book I stuck under the front page of the *India Abroad*.

"What are you reading?"

"Nothing," I say again, pushing the Bernstein book out of sight. So far, I haven't told him about Shanthi's play. I'm not sure why, but I don't want to talk about it just yet. I want to hold on to my secret just a little longer.

He goes back to his crossword. Then: "You're singing."

"I'm not!"

"You're humming." He studies me. "There's something . . . different."

"Everyone hums," I say. On my iPod, the song "Something's Coming" is getting louder, and with effort, I try not to mouth the words that I already know.

By now, Mrs. Carmichael (*diabetes, multigrain flour*) has come into the store. "Is your father here?" she asks me.

"Yeah, just a minute." I don't see Dad in the aisle, so I go to the back room, where I find him and our accountant, Aasif, huddled together. Their faces are motionless and grim.

"You have to hold off," Aasif (*gold-rimmed glasses, numbers, cricket*) says. He glances at his computer, where a spreadsheet is open. "I don't think you can get it replaced this month."

"That refrigerator is ten years old," Dad says. "It's on its last legs." His face is worn, and I notice now he's wearing the same shirt as yesterday. It's a dark shade of gray, and I recognize the turmeric stain on the sleeve.

"You need to stretch over into next month after you've paid the rent," Aasif says carefully, like my dad is a loose cannon and the wrong words will set him off. But that's not my dad. He's *hard work, reminds, repeats*. Not someone who loses control. Or is he?

He notices me standing there. "What do you need, Karthu?"

"Mrs. Carmichael wants to talk to you," I say.

Dad hurries out to greet her.

"Is it too expensive to fix the refrigerator?" I ask Aasif. I don't know why, but my heart is pounding. From the doorway I see Dad laughing and talking to Mrs. Carmichael. But his back is hunched the way it gets when he's watching cricket and India is getting its "clock cleaned."

"It's too expensive to run the store," Aasif says, then sees my face. "Don't worry," he adds quickly. But he isn't convincing.

Aasif is one of those people who knows everything. My mom thinks he was a prince in a previous life. I don't know about that. But he's the one who explained cricket to me. He's good with numbers and knows when a distributor is ripping us off or who has the best deal. He knows about rates of return on investments and how to arrange okra in the bin so the old ones get bought first. And now he says the store is too expensive to run. Isn't that another way of saying we'll go out of business? I want to ask him if my deliveries are helping, but I'm too chicken.

As we're talking, my eyes fall on the hand vacuum cleaner hanging on the wall. Seeing it reminds me of one time when I was over at Miles's apartment. "Can we try something?" I ask Aasif. "But you need to help me."

"Sure thing, Captain," he says. Then he helps me move the refrigerators away from the wall.

"Miles's dad said sometimes the back needs to be cleaned and then it starts working again."

"This is what you kids do for fun? What happened to basketball and football?"

I shrug. "I can't throw. Neither can Miles." I start up the hand vac.

"What's going on?" a customer asks. "Is the refrigerator broken?"

"No, no," Aasif says. "Just some housecleaning." His gold spectacles flash in the sunlight as he watches me. Dad comes over and asks Aasif what we're doing, and Aasif explains to him in a whisper while I vacuum the entire backs of the refrigerators until all the fuzz and lint are gone.

As the three customers in the store hover around, Dad repeats, "Nothing's wrong," with his Grocery Smile plastered on.

Hearing my dad makes my stomach hurt, like a hundred butterflies are trapped in there. *The refrigerator is breaking. The customers are dwindling. The vegetables are being thrown out.* Then I go through Carmine's fifty flavors in my head to stop myself from thinking of all the reasons the store will fail.

But as the morning goes by, the pool of water doesn't return and the refrigerators are working like before. Meanwhile, the phone rings off the hook in the nearly empty store, and Dad writes down all the deliveries for me, even when I tell him not to.

A danger has been averted. At least for now.

HISTORY OF LENNY BERNSTEIN IN 6 PARTS

- Born in Lawrence, MA. Raised in Allston, Roxbury, Newton.
- His dad owns a beauty salon (100x worse than a grocery store—sorry, I wouldn't want my dad selling wigs). Wants his son to go into the business, but Lenny wants to play the piano.
- Everybody thinks Lenny is talented. He plays the piano, goes to Harvard. Girls want to marry him. His dad is like, okay, you can be a musician.
- Becomes conductor of the New York Philharmonic. Then everyone is like, "We love Lenny!"
- Gets married, has kids, becomes wildly famous. Writes *West Side Story* and other music.
- Gets old and wonders if he's done enough. Wonders if being a conductor is enough. What about the piano? What about writing more music? Dies five years before I'm born.

Chapter 5

The next morning, we have no vegetables. We wait but the delivery truck doesn't come. So I tell Dad I'm going to CVS to get a notebook. He's on the phone with the distributor and he's busy shouting, so he waves me off with his hand and I'm out the door. Then what I actually do is go to Carmine's, where I order two scoops of Caramel Swirl and read about Lenny.

The way I see it, I have no choice. Every day it seems like something new and bad is happening. First it's the refrigerator. Now it's the delivery truck. What kind of grocery store doesn't have vegetables to sell? At this rate, the store will be doomed before the month is over.

So I do the only thing I can think of doing when I'm worried. I eat ice cream and read.

I learn about Lenny's life. Turns out he was good at memorizing, too. He memorized piano music so he could play at parties and people's houses and performance halls. He memorized entire scores of orchestral pieces before he conducted. Is that why he was a genius? For remembering all those notes? He was a composer, too. He wrote the music for *West Side Story*, but he wrote other things, too, like whole symphonies and music for orchestras and singers.

As I read about him, I try to figure out what Shanthi sees in me that reminds her of Lenny.

5 WAYS THAT LENNY IS LIKE ME

- Curly, goofy hair
- Memorizes stuff
- Close to his sister (okay, a stretch)
- Frail and skinny and the big kids chased him
- Son of immigrants

In 1932, Lenny was the same age as me now. I try to imagine Allston back then. Were there cable cars? Did the T run on Comm Ave? It was during the Great Depression, when people were out of work. I study Lenny's face in the photos to see if he's worried that his father's salon will go under, that customers will stop coming to the store to buy wigs or get their hair curled. But Lenny's smiling like he's looking forward, not backward, like he knows it will all work out and someday he'll be famous. That's one way Lenny is not like me.

Suddenly I feel something icy cold drip on my arm. "Aargh!" I yelp.

"God, I'm so sorry!" It's Juhi.

Wow, I didn't see her come in. I'm so surprised I can't even hide my book.

"My cones always leak. It's like this talent I have. Here." She gives me one of her napkins for my arm and then before I can stop her, she picks up my book from the table. "*A Man of Many Talents: The Life of Bernstein*. Cool. As in Leonard Bernstein?"

How does she know who he is?

"I'm reading it for a friend," I say, taking the book from her. I wipe off my arm. "Well, not a friend. More like a customer. I mean, I didn't pick it out. And . . . uh, did you order Everything?"

She nods. "Yep. It's Everything. You?"

"Caramel Swirl. The usual." I don't know why I add that when she doesn't even know what's usual for me. My brain races to think of something else to say. "You want to see something cool?"

"Sure," she says. She slurps the bottom of her cone.

I flip through the pages of the book. "See this photo? It's back in the 1930s. But it's *here*."

She looks interested. "You mean Carmine's?"

"No, not the ice cream shop. Allston." I guess it would be cooler if it *was* a photo of Carmine's. But the ice cream shop isn't that old.

Still, it seems to work, because Juhi sits down across from me, her cone dripping onto the table. "Whoa! It's Comm Ave. With a Model T car!" She flips through the pages.

"Yeah, I know," I say. I try not to stare, but there's this thing about her hair, something I've noticed since we were little, how the ends line up perfectly. I couldn't even cut paper that straight. In kindergarten, I used to think her hair was magic. I was always getting in trouble for pulling Juhi Shah's hair. Even now, it's hard not to touch it, just to see if the ends will mess up—though I have a feeling they wouldn't.

She's now slurping and eating her ice cream cone from the bottom up. I've never seen anyone eat their ice cream that way. "You can keep reading if you want," she says and slides the book back to me.

"Nah," I say. Lenny can wait.

"So why are you reading this again?"

I hesitate. I haven't even told Miles about Shanthi's play. But Juhi is looking at me and suddenly I find myself telling her all about it.

"She wants me to play Lenny," I say when I'm done.

"You? Wow."

"Yeah." It does sound pretty amazing.

"In front of people? Have you ever acted before?"

"Uh, no." That part doesn't sound so amazing. I clear my throat. "Well, I said I'd think about it."

"My mom's friend is an actor," Juhi says. "He lives in New York City."

"Really?"

"He does stuff on Broadway. He's got an agent."

I'm not sure what an agent does, but I nod anyway. I've never been to a Broadway show. Come to think of it, I've never been to *any* show. Nitya wanted to see *Les Misérables* at the Boston Opera House, but Mom said the tickets were too expensive.

"He's been doing small gigs," Juhi says. "Nothing huge."

"Yeah, it's tough being an actor."

Juhi takes another bite of her cone. "Plus, he's Indian."

"So?"

"Well, you know. Indian guys don't have a chance. They aren't . . ." She stops, probably because she realizes she's talking to one.

I continue eating my ice cream in silence. What was Juhi going to say? But I think I already know. It helps having a sister who calls you Dweeb.

4 WAYS THAT INDIAN GUYS "AREN'T"

- Uncool
- Wrong haircut
- Wear clothes their uncool moms buy (hello, Target)
- Can program their computer but not their social life

The thing is, if Juhi thinks this way, it's totally unfair. It's like saying if you're an Indian guy, you don't have a chance at life.

"Can I look at that again?" Juhi asks, taking the book from me. "I've seen *West Side Story*."

"Sure," I say.

Juhi starts reading the first page, maybe because she's embarrassed that she said Indian guys *aren't*. Or maybe she's actually interested. I wait for her to close the book, but she keeps reading. She turns the page.

I finish my bowl of Caramel Swirl and watch her. "Just your average child prodigy," I say.

"Hmm," she says.

Great. So she'd rather read about a dead musician than talk to me.

I watch her some more and I forget about why Indian Guys Aren't. Instead, I remember all the things I've liked about Juhi. In kindergarten, it was her hair ends matching up. In first grade, it was her sweater with the butterfly buttons. Then it was a bubblegum smell—maybe it was the shampoo she used. She smelled like bubblegum for a long time. Then she stopped, but by then I liked something else—the way she said *righto!* And so, I guess this list makes me pathetic. But now I like her because even if all the other girls in our grade have turned mean, Juhi is the only one who smiles at me. And, maybe because she's Indian, she has never ever called me Kar-dick.

"Shanthi says I look like Lenny," I tell her. And that I'm a genius! But I don't say that. In fact, I don't even know why I said that part about looking like him. It sounds like I'm bragging, when I'm not. It's the only thing I can think of, and I want to keep talking to her.

Juhi studies the front cover of *Lenny* and then me.

"Not when he's old!" I exclaim.

She giggles and it's nice, and then I don't feel like an "Indian guy" anymore. I feel like me. Maybe Juhi's never had that list in her head and it's me being paranoid because of Nitya.

Juhi flips through the rest of the pages to a photo of Lenny when he's in grade school. "Hey, she's right. It's the hair." She reaches over to push my bangs to one side. "Now you're Lenny."

No one has touched my hair before. No one except my mom, but she doesn't count. I want to look around to see if anyone is watching, but I don't.

"So, how do you know all the flavors at Carmine's?" I ask, changing the subject to show I'm fine, like girls rearrange my hair all the time. "You must have a good memory." I wait for her to say yes, so we can have something huge in common to bond over.

"No, my sister worked at Carmine's last summer in Brookline. She had to memorize the flavors, and I helped. Free ice cream, right?" Well, at least we can bond over ice cream. "Do you have a good memory?" she asks. "Or you just like ice cream?" Her hair falls in straight lines as she talks. I wish there was something about me that perfect.

"No," I say. "I just like ice cream." I like the way that sounds, like I'm normal.

Her eyes flicker past me to the front door. I turn around and it's Jacob Donnell. This time he's alone. "Um, listen, I have to go," she says. "I wanted to . . . ask Jacob something."

By now Jacob has seen us, and he nods at Juhi. When did that happen? They never hung out at school, and now, what, they're together?

Juhi gets up. Then I guess she feels bad, because she says, "Tell me how the play goes, okay?"

"Yeah," I say, even though who cares.

She walks to the counter where Jacob is standing. I can't hear what they say, but a few moments later, Juhi orders another Everything cone, as if she hadn't just eaten one already with me. *She'll be sick*, I think. *She'll barf from all that ice cream, and it will be right in front of Jacob Donnell, and he'll be so grossed out he'll stop talking to her, and it won't matter because he's a butthead.*

Just then my phone rings. "Sweet motherland of India, where are you?" Dad's voice rings across the phone line. I see he's called a few times and I didn't notice while I was talking to Juhi.

"Sorry."

"When someone calls in with a delivery, we need to get it to them right away. It does no good to deliver something hours later."

"I thought the delivery truck didn't come," I say stonily.

"It did! I have a bag packed already for Mrs. Gupta. Don't delay."

After I hang up, Jacob and Juhi are still eating ice cream and talking. If Juhi feels sick to her stomach from her second cone, it doesn't show. Instead, she's giggly and hair-flippy, and she's definitely not eating her cone from the bottom either. I guess that's the difference between being the most popular boy in school and being me. I'm the one who gets ice cream dripped on him.

On my way out, Jacob calls out, "Yo, Kar-dick," his suntanned face turned up under his Red Sox cap. As usual, it's like a punch in the gut.

Then Juhi smiles at me, her fingers going back and forth in a half wave, and that little thing lifts me up. It reminds me we talked for real, that I didn't imagine it.

Outside Carmine's, I push my hair to one side like Juhi did. It doesn't make me Jacob Donnell. It doesn't make me Lenny. But it does make me happy.

7 REASONS TO BE IN SHANTHI'S PLAY

- It would piss off my mom (if I told her)
- Girl magnet (Juhi)
- Good use of my memorizing skills
- Good on my college application (Really?)
- More fun than delivering mangos
- Shanthi thinks I can do it
- What if I can?

Chapter 6

The next day, I run into Miles, who's standing in front of McDougal's Liquor Store. "Dude, they'll never let you in there," I tease him.

"I'm noticing," he says, ignoring me, "how the price of beer has gone down." He points to the sale signs plastered over the windows. "This is the second week Heineken is on sale. It's cheaper than Budweiser. That *never* happens."

"So what?" I say. I look at my reflection in the window to see if my hair is still pushed to one side. "Spencer can't afford Heineken?"

"Spencer?" Miles repeats his brother's name. "This is no joke. It's the *economy*."

"Oh," I say. I'm sick of the economy. Now Miles is talking about it, too.

I push my hair some more, but it seems to have a mind of its own. *You look like a goonda*, Mom had told me this morning when she said I needed a haircut. As if thugs have floppy hair and deliver groceries.

Miles glances at the back of my bike. "How many more deliveries do you have?"

"A few."

He follows me to Harvard Ave. There's a line of people in front of House of Chaat.

"What's going on?" He looks at the sign. "What's chaat? It sounds Indian."

"It is," I say. "It's snack food, like samosas." Miles loves those, but we only have the frozen kind at the store that we have to heat up in the microwave.

He pushes up his glasses. "Cool. Let's go in."

"I can't or my dad will kill me. I was already late today." I wheel my bike around the line of people and we keep walking. "Why do you care about the price of beer?"

"I've got a bad feeling."

"About beer?"

Miles doesn't say anything.

"About your brother?"

"About my dad. What if he loses his job? That's all he's been talking about."

When he says that, it's like Miles is talking about *my* dad. I feel the same butterflies in my stomach again. "Your dad's a plumber, right? Plumbers don't go out of business. Isn't there always a toilet backing up or something?"

"My dad doesn't fix toilets," Miles says sharply.

Yikes. Wrong thing to say. Though if you think about it, what's wrong with fixing toilets? Lenny's dad sold wigs. Mine sells mangos. It all evens out.

"My Uncle Milton is a plumber, and *he* lost his job. I don't want my dad to be next."

"Right," I say. I don't want my dad to be next either.

HISTORY OF DAD'S STORE IN 6 PARTS

- Opens in Allston where Comm Ave bends.
- Called "Indian Groceries" because no one has any better ideas.
- Aasif hired to manage the books.
- Space expands from one aisle to two to three.
- Wall Street crashes and a family member (me) has to deliver groceries for free.
- Hoping we survive the summer.

At 6:00 P.M. after we close up the store, my dad and I stop at the deli next door to buy a lottery ticket. Dad does this a few times a week and chats with Mr. Miller. When we walk over, we see Mr. Miller is putting up a sign in the front window. "Giant Sale. 50% off everything!"

"That *is* a giant sale," Dad says when we're inside.

Mr. Miller finishes hanging up his sign and comes over to the cash register.

"Here for your lottery ticket, Manjesh?" he asks. "The usual or something different?"

"Yes, the usual," Dad says. "I like routine."

We both wait for Mr. Miller to say something about the sign. Dad is too polite to be the one to ask. As Mr. Miller rings up the lottery ticket, Dad hands him a one-dollar bill.

"Retiring," Mr. Miller finally says.

"What's that, Lyon?"

"I'm retiring early," he says. "I'm moving to Florida. Got a condo in Naples near my daughter. It's a good time to close the shop. Before it gets ugly here."

Dad looks surprised. "Lyon. I'm sorry!"

"Oh no." Mr. Miller shakes his head. "It's a blessing. I get to see my grandkids. And it's better I leave before I'm run out, right?" He smiles, a gold crown flashing at the back of his mouth.

Mr. Miller has been around literally forever. I remember getting candy from him when Nitya and I were little and would stop by with Dad. It was weird candy—hard striped ones that tasted like ginger. Nitya and I would spit them out after we left. But it was still nice of him, I guess.

"Hope you catch a break with this one," Mr. Miller says, handing the ticket to Dad. "Hey, you're getting big, aren't you, Karson," he says to me.

"Thanks," I say. That's another thing. In all the years I've known him, Mr. Miller has never gotten my name right.

Dad holds the door open for me. "Come on, Karson," he says.

♪

When we get on the T to go home, it's super hot inside. That's when I notice the windows are all open in the compartment, which means the air-conditioning isn't working. Even though the T runs aboveground from here until we get home, we'll still be roasting. Great.

I watch Dad scratch his lottery ticket. He looks at the four numbers: 3–4–8–9.

"Didn't I get these numbers yesterday?" he asks.

"No. Yesterday was 2–4–6–9."

"Really? Oh well." Dad tucks the ticket into his shirt pocket. He never wins, but that won't stop him from buying another lottery ticket at Mr. Miller's the next time. "The universe is lucky if you can find the luck," he adds. He always says that, too. Dad has high hopes for the universe. I wonder where he will buy his ticket after Mr. Miller leaves. I wonder if Dad is wondering the same thing.

My iPod battery is drained, so I'm listening to the subway tracks going underneath us. Not exactly music. We're almost at Warren Street when the T sputters along for a few moments and then stops completely. We're stuck between two stations. Everyone in the car groans.

"Why don't we just walk home," I grumble. "It would take less time."

"We'll be up and running soon," Dad says.

I finger the window. Around us, people are restless. It's getting hotter as we wait.

"Why do you think the price of beer has gone down?" I ask.

Dad looks at me. "Why would you know that?"

"Miles noticed the prices outside McDougal's."

Dad makes a *tsk-tsk* sound. "McDougal's is the last place he ought to be hanging around. I should watch you both more carefully. Even if Miles's parents should be doing that."

"Oh, forget it," I say angrily. Why does he have to be a pain?

Dad lets out his breath. "All right, why do you care if the price of beer has gone down?"

An announcement on the loudspeaker says we'll be moving soon, but we all know the score.

"Yeah, right," someone says.

"Is it because of the Financial Crisis?" I ask. "Miles thinks his dad could lose his job."

"What does he do?"

"He's a plumber."

Dad considers this for a moment. "These days, anything can happen."

"Why? What's wrong with the economy? Is that why Mr. Miller is leaving?"

Dad looks out the window, where the light is starting to change in the sky. "Well, there were banks lending money to people who couldn't pay them back. And there were people on Wall Street cheating the system and making lots of money from it. That ended up affecting all of us."

"Mom says a lot of people are out of work."

"That's right."

"Are we in trouble, too?" I ask.

Dad shifts. "We shouldn't be afraid to take chances. The universe will come through for us."

How can he be so positive? He already lost his job once in Albuquerque.

"But will we be okay?"

"I'm not going to lie," he says. "It's a bad time. But I've been through bad times before. When I was a young boy in India, my family owned rice fields. It was a good life. We had our own cow and fresh milk. We had our own rice. But it was also very hard. My dad—your thatha—had to work long hours. Oversee workers. Every day he had to be in the field. Some years we had too much rain, some years we had drought. But he got through it. We will get through this like Thatha did. With hard work. It's about doing your best. Showing up, Karthu." Dad pauses. "If I can count on you to do those deliveries, we can get to the end of the summer. Then who knows, in September, we can hire more people and buy more bikes!"

Count on me? Since when has anyone done that?

The lights turn on in the train as the engine whirs back to life.

"See?" Dad says. "The universe is up and running. You just have to trust it."

He smiles, but I see the worry in his eyes. This summer might be our last chance between succeeding or failing. And I know then what I have to do.

HOW TO SAVE DAD'S STORE

- Make as many deliveries as I can.
- Don't get distracted.
- Don't get flat tires.
- Don't be in Shanthi's play. Don't.

Chapter 7

I even know how I'll say it to her: *You can keep your twenty dollars.* Only, I'll talk like Matt Damon in *Good Will Hunting*, so it will sound more like *dollas*. No big deal. Then why am I so nervous?

When I get to Shanthi's apartment, she buzzes me in and we sit down at her table with the bag of chips and Fanta she'd ordered. For a few minutes, we eat and talk about stuff. She tells me she studied economics in college, then in her last year she decided she wanted to be a writer. BU had a playwriting program, so she applied and got in.

"What did your parents say?" I ask. I wonder what my parents would do if one day in college I decide to do something different, like basket-weaving or parachute-jumping or whatever.

"They flipped. They thought I would work on Wall Street."

"Whoa," I say. "So you walked away from all that."

"I'm SO glad I did. I'm so glad I'm not on Wall Street."

"Because of the Financial Crisis?" There it is again, the recession. It's like my mom is in the room. But if she was, she'd be warning me about Shanthi. Don't get any ideas, Cutie!

"Because it's better to make my own choices. Even if my mom doesn't like them."

"That's right. She's not talking to you."

"You don't forget anything, do you?" Shanthi finishes the last of the spicy chips and throws the bag away in the garbage can. "So," she says meaningfully.

My stomach twinges. "Yeah, I read the Bernstein book."

"And?"

"He seems pretty cool."

"Pretty cool?"

"I guess everyone thought he was a genius. Good grades at Boston Latin School. Then learning the piano, studying at the New England Conservatory, going to Harvard, and being a world-famous conductor. And oh yeah, writing *West Side Story*."

"Wow, Lenny's life, summarized in two sentences."

I think for a moment. "Actually, four sentences."

She lets out her breath. "Oh man."

"I just know it was four."

"Okay, but aside from his life in thirty seconds. Does he make you stop in your tracks?"

I blink. "What do you mean?"

"Does he speak to you? Like, could you get to the heart of him?"

I'm feeling queasy. It's time to do my Matt Damon line. *You can keep your twenty dollas.*

Shanthi gets up from her chair and goes to a closet behind her. She returns with a softbound book. This isn't a library book—it looks like it was bound at Staples. "It's finally done," she says. She doesn't tell me what the book is. But I know. And I know why she has it in her hand. To give to me.

"I can't be in your play," I blurt out. There. I've said it.

Shanthi looks at me, the book held against her chest. What will she do? Throw me out? It doesn't matter. Other than the deliveries, I'll never have to talk to her again.

"Why? Is something wrong?

"I just can't," I say. "You know, fraternizing isn't allowed." I read somewhere that when you have customers, you don't get involved in their lives. It's called fraternizing. I try to sound all official and hope she can't tell that I don't know what I'm talking about.

"You're not fraternizing. I'm hiring you."

"Then I can't moonlight. You can keep your twenty—"

"Moonlight as a delivery boy?" Shanthi interrupts. "Okay, what's the real reason?"

"I don't know how to act. I'll probably stink at it."

"I'll teach you."

"And . . ." I look away. "My dad needs me at the store." *This summer is our last chance.*

"I told you, we'll work around your schedule. Like today. I'll order groceries. Then you come and practice for ten minutes. I'll keep ordering stuff. So it's good for your store, too."

I don't say anything. *Just say no*, I tell myself. *Dad's counting on you.*

"Don't you see? You won't be a kid. You'll be an actor. It's how you see yourself."

"Well, maybe I don't see myself as an actor," I say.

"What do you see yourself as? A delivery boy?"

The truth is, I don't see myself as anything. It's my mom who's always saying I'll be a doctor. I just go along because I don't have any better ideas. Still, that has nothing to do with what this is about. This is about my dad and hard work and his dad and hard work. About my thatha working long hours in the rice fields and having his own cow and fresh milk for his family. It's about my dad not losing his job and me helping him. I think.

Shanthi holds out the homemade book. "Here's your chance to do something *unexpected*. When I saw you, I knew you'd be the perfect Lenny."

As she speaks, there it is, the ping I felt before. I think of my dad, and it's weird how there's a composite of memories I have of him, all superimposed on one another: my dad in Albuquerque crying when he lost his computer job, my dad opening the grocery store for the first time, him giving Nitya and me lollipops and Fanta, him and me putting up signs in the display window, and now us in the store, hoping and wondering and waiting to see how it all turns out.

But does my dad counting on me mean I can't do anything else?

"If I do it, I can't be late for my deliveries," I say slowly. Am I really saying that? It's like a chorus of little me's are in my head yelling, *No, No, No!*

"You won't be," Shanthi says. "I'll make sure." She seems to believe I can be Lenny, like the impossible can happen to me.

"And I don't know how to act. I'll screw it all up."

"You won't." She holds out the book to me. "Do the unexpected."

Do the unexpected.

I know I should say no.

INSTANCES OF ME NOT SAYING NO

- When I had to wear Nitya's hand-me-down pants with butterflies on the pockets
- When Miles asked me to eat a worm
- When Mom made me read about bone glue and open-heart surgery
- When Dad asked me to work in the store all summer

But what if this isn't about when to say no but when to say yes?

I take the script from Shanthi, and I feel it again, a pinging in my chest. I look at the top:

```
BEING LENNY
A Play in One Act
by Shanthi Ananth
Boston University, 2009
```

"Shanthi Ananth," I say. "That's your name?"

"I thought you knew already."

"I didn't know your last name." My phone rings.

"Wow, he doesn't stop, does he?"

"No. But sometimes I ignore him."

"Like now?"

"Like now."

"You are going to be an awesome actor. I can just feel it in my bones," she says.

"You are a very weird person, Shanthi Ananth."

She laughs. "I know."

I feel that strange mixture of excitement and terror you get when you're about to do something you've never done before. The last time I felt this way was when my family and I drove to Six Flags and I rode the Cyclone roller coaster and barfed afterward. I hope being Lenny will be better than that.

Chapter 8

The rest of the day I barely have time to breathe. One person wants a twenty-pound bag of basmati rice that makes my bike wobble as I peddle. Another customer asks for a whole bunch of frozen groceries that need to be rushed to her before the frozen coconut starts thawing. Mr. Jain accidentally dropped his box of tea in a pot of boiling water and needs a new box as soon as possible along with some more frozen samosas. Another pair of mangos are exchanged for Mrs. Rodrigues. Up and down Comm Ave, I deliver groceries all afternoon.

Shanthi's script is stored in my bicycle crate, and between deliveries, I manage to pull it out for a few moments. The first line reads: *Nobody will believe me when I tell them, I knew about this.* Lenny's talking about when the piano arrives in his home for the first time, and he knows he's going to be famous. I don't know how he knows. He just does.

All day I whisper those words to myself: *I knew about this.*

In the evening, Miles comes over to watch *Star Trek*. We sit in front of the TV with microwave popcorn and Fanta while my mom and sister are yelling in the hallway about who's cleaning the bathroom—Nitya, or my mom, the "resident maid" (my mom's idea of humor).

"I remember this episode," Miles says. "It's where they try to blow up the *Enterprise*."

I ask him what his favorite episode is. Miles isn't sure and he asks me, and I give him my top five, which excludes the *Voyager* season (because it sucked) and *Deep Space Nine*, which I haven't seen. I watch as Miles guzzles down some Fanta. "Your dad okay?" I ask.

He wipes his mouth with the back of his hand. "What? Yeah. Whatever."

This seems like a good sign. His dad can't be out of a job with that *whatever* thrown in. So I say, "It's because of the Financial Crisis. My dad was saying how with the economy, banks made bad decisions, and . . ."

"You didn't tell him about my dad, did you?" Miles's voice goes up a notch.

Oops. I give him my best of-course-not look. "Of course not," I say.

We go back to eating popcorn and watching *Star Trek*.

"So how come you're reading about Leonard Bernstein?" Miles asks.

I almost choke on my popcorn. "How did you know?" I look to see if my script is lying around somewhere, but the only thing on the coffee table is the *Boston Globe*.

"I saw the book you were reading at the store. Why, is it a secret?"

I decide then that if Juhi knows, it's okay for Miles to know, too. So I tell him about Shanthi's play.

"But dude," Miles says. "You don't act."

"I can learn the lines."

"Isn't acting more than knowing your lines?"

Is Miles dissing the whole thing? I guess I look annoyed because he tries to be nice.

"Sounds cool," he says. He pushes up his glasses. "Your parents know?"

"I'll tell them later," I say, though basically my plan is to never tell them if I can help it. I already know my dad is stressed out about the store and wouldn't want me to take time away from my deliveries to rehearse. And I don't want to tell my mom either. She'll say it's a waste of time, that we should stick to things we're good at, that nobody she's ever known is an actor. My dad would kill me with the delivery schedule. But my mom is where dreams go to die.

That night, Miles sleeps over.

"Do you think you can know what you're going to be?" I ask from my bed. Miles is in a sleeping bag on the floor.

"What do you mean? Nobody knows what they're going to be."

I look into the darkness, which isn't truly dark, because I can see the outlines of everything, and there's moonlight filtering through the curtains. "In Shanthi's play, Lenny does. He sounds like he knows he'll be famous someday."

"That's just a play," Miles says. "She probably wrote him like that to be interesting. Writers do that kind of stuff all the time."

"I think Lenny knew."

"Maybe. But if it were me, I wouldn't want to know."

"You wouldn't want to know what?"

"What's going to happen in my life. I'd rather just see what happens."

I sat up. "You wouldn't want to know if you're going to be famous?"

"You want to be famous?"

"I want to know what I'm going to be," I say. I think of Lenny standing in front of the New York Philharmonic. I think of the ping in my chest when Shanthi said I could be in her play, or my favorite line, *I knew about this*, and how I like to say it under my breath when I'm riding my bike on Comm Ave. But mostly I think of bone glue and beating hearts and how my mom might be the smartest person I know, even smarter than Miles. But can't she get it wrong sometimes, too?

"Because if you know you're going to be really good at something," I say to Miles, "you don't have to worry about it ever."

Miles pulls up the front of his sleeping bag so that only his eyes and nose show in the moonlight. Then he asks, "Why do you have to worry about it at all?"

HOW TO BE SUCCESSFUL

- Know what you want to be before anyone else in your family decides for you.
- Talk to people in the know (like Shanthi).
- Know what you're good at. But know your flaws, too (like my front tooth is chipped).
- Make a plan. This one's hard. I literally have no idea. Yet.
- Tell yourself you're going to do it. Whatever IT is.
- Make lists so you don't forget.

Chapter 9

My sister can't dance. If we all came to this conclusion, it would save my family a lot of time and money. Instead, my mom insists on dragging us to Nitya's dance performance, where she puts on gobs of makeup and stumbles around onstage with a bunch of other girls who can't dance either.

"I don't want him there," Nitya says. "He sits in the front and makes faces. It ruins my concentration."

"That was when I was ten. Geez." Now that she mentions it though, it isn't a bad idea.

Mom is firm. "We're all going. Even Raj."

"Wait, why Raj?" Nitya asks.

"Pavan and Hema are driving to Maine for a wedding," Mom explains. "They're leaving right after the performance. We're taking Raj home with us after the dance."

I groan. "Man, can this day get any worse?"

Mom shoots off instructions. "Cutie, put on your silk kurta. Baby, stand still, or how can I braid your hair?"

"I can braid it myself," Nitya whines. "You always make it too tight."

I leave them to find a place to hide the silk kurta because:

- It's like wearing pajamas in public.
- Silk is actually "raw silk." Meaning: itchy.
- My dad and I hate them.
- Mom buys them every time she visits India.
- Then she wonders, *Why do they keep vanishing?*

I'm considering putting it under my bed, when my mom suddenly grows X-ray eyes.

"Don't you stuff it under your bed," she calls from Nitya's room.

Twenty minutes later, we're in the car, perspiring and itchy.

"Stop buying these," Dad barks. He fingers the collar around his neck.

My mother is unperturbed. "You both look so nice. So sharp."

Nitya gazes at me. "Dweeb," she says. She looks scary with all that makeup on her face, her eyes outlined with kajal.

"You look like a raccoon," I say.

"I hope you trip in that kurta," she says.

My mother glares at us from the front seat. "Be nice. This is a big evening for Baby."

"Stop calling me that," Nitya says. "I'm seventeen."

"What would you guys say if I wanted to learn the piano?" I ask casually.

"What?" Mom says. "Oh, Cutie. We tried that already. Baby failed."

"I didn't *fail*," Nitya says. "I started high school. I don't have time to practice."

"Three years of dust collecting on that keyboard," Dad observes.

"At least we didn't pour money into a real piano," Mom says.

"Harder to dust," Dad says.

He and Mom laugh.

I've predicted this entire conversation.

"Yeah, way too expensive," I agree. "What if I wanted to try acting lessons?"

It's called planting seeds. In English class, Mrs. Dubois told us if you want your audience to believe a twist in your story, you have to plant the seeds for it early on. You can't spring surprises at the end. I figure I can plant a few ideas of my own. Next to my sister's dusty keyboard, anything else I ask for will seem reasonable, right?

Mom turns around again, the evening light sparkling on her neck. She's wearing either a diamond necklace or a fake. It's hard to tell with Indian jewelry. "What are you talking about?" she asks me.

"The Dweeb acting, ha ha," Nitya says, giggling. "He can't even sing."

"Oh, it's a joke." Mom looks at the road and yells at my dad for almost sideswiping an SUV.

"You already act like a dork," Nitya says. "No lessons required."

So much for planting seeds.

♪

For some mysterious reason, the auditorium is always crowded at these performances. Who would willingly watch my sister and her goon friends dance? Unless you come for the food. Not that eating partially reheated channa masala and aloo gobi made by the auntie moms is worth the pain of being stuck here for hours. But nothing else makes sense.

When we get there, I see Raj (*giant*, *clown*) standing with some kids near the front of the auditorium. My cousin looks the way he always does—like a large, sprawling mess. No one knows why Raj is so gigantic, with huge, beefy arms and rippling leg muscles, when his parents are so small and twiggy. But so far, Raj's size seems to help him. He plays every varsity sport in high school, and let's just say he isn't the kind of person who got his pants pulled down during recess. The depantsers probably ran when they saw him. But that doesn't make me want to hang out with him. So I sit far away on one of the foldout chairs in the audience while my parents are mingling with some of the other parents near the food table on the other side of the auditorium.

A priest goes up to a microphone onstage. "Good evening, everyone. Welcome to a night of spiritual enlightenment and artistic entertainment."

The crowd subsides to muffled whispers while the aunties in the back keep talking. My mom and dad quickly take seats near the food.

I'm glad they don't sit near me. I open my backpack and pull out Shanthi's play. Without them nearby, no one will care if I'm not watching my sister stumble around onstage for god knows how long. Dance recitals have a way of making you reevaluate your life. And not in a good way.

I decide to start again from the beginning of the play. I'd read about half yesterday, but I kept getting interrupted with so many deliveries.

CHARACTERS
Leonard "Lenny" Bernstein
Sam Bernstein (father)
Jennie Bernstein (mother)

SET
Play opens with morning light filtering through window. LENNY is in the living room of his apartment, standing in front of a piano. STREET NOISE in background.

SCENE 1
LENNY: (to audience) Nobody will believe me when I tell them, I *knew* about this. (He leans forward to stroke a few keys.)

(Offstage SAM calls to LENNY)

SAM: Lenny, don't touch that piano.

LENNY: I was at Aunt Clara's. I didn't know what I was doing, but I was able to pick out "Good Night, Sweetheart." (plays some more) She's a kook, but she likes me. I know that's why she sent us the piano. Because of *me*.

SAM: Lenny, away from the piano! Hundred times I have to tell you!

```
(Offstage JENNIE calls to LENNY).

JENNIE: Lenny, breakfast! Come—the
morning waits for no one!

LENNY: (conspiratorial) I knew
something was coming, something good,
and . . . it's here!
```

Then, as I'm reading, three things happen:

- the curtains open
- the music blares
- a big splat of channa masala lands on me

"I'm sorry," Juhi wails. "The music made me jump."

"What are you doing here?" I ask, staring at her. She's standing next to me in the aisle with a plate of flatbread and partially reheated channa masala.

Juhi nods toward the stage and says something I can't hear over the music.

"What?" I ask.

"MY SISTER," she says loudly.

"Sit down," someone says behind us. "You're blocking."

Juhi sits down in an empty seat next to me. The channa masala has soaked through the front page of Shanthi's script, with a glop of chickpeas stuck in the middle. Juhi uses a napkin to wipe off the food, but it only makes the stain bigger. "I'm sorry," she says again.

I tell her it's okay while the same person who made the blocking comment says, "Sshh!" in a loud, obnoxious way. "You should be watching your sisters," she says sternly. She's dressed in a bright red sari with big, sparkly jewelry hanging from her neck and ears, but she still looks like a cow.

We watch for a while as Juhi finishes her bread and channa masala, then she whispers to me, "This is boring."

"I know," I whisper back. The music is so loud we can't talk. Then I have this thought. "You want to walk around upstairs?" I ask.

She brightens. "Sure," she says.

I see Raj looking back from his seat just as we walk out the door. I wonder if my parents saw me, too. They might get pissed that I'm missing Nitya's performance. But I'm doing what she wanted me to in the first place. Who knows, Nitya might dance better if she wasn't distracted by the sight of me.

Chapter 10

We're barefoot in the temple above the auditorium, because you aren't supposed to walk inside with your shoes. The white marble floor feels smooth and cool under my feet.

Juhi says, "Should we be here? Maybe we'll get in trouble."

I look at the stone deities surrounding us: Ganesha, Lakshmi, Venkateswara.

"Nah," I say. I don't know for sure, but I don't want to leave yet.

Juhi sits down on the marble floor. "Let's read the play," she says.

We start from the beginning until we get to the part with the channa masala stain. "I'm so sorry!" she says again.

"That's okay. It's the end of the scene."

"Look—this sounds like *West Side Story*!" She points to a line.

```
LENNY: (conspiratorial) I knew
something was coming, something good,
and . . . it's here!
```

"Tony sings something like that before he meets Maria," Juhi says.

"You mean 'Something's Coming'?" I sing the opening words to the song, my voice echoing inside the hall. I've never heard myself this way, like I'm hearing someone else but I know it's me.

"You're good," she says. "You should try out for the school musical."

I flush. "Really? Thanks."

"I wanted to be in the play last year, but my parents said no. Remember my mom's friend I was telling you about?"

"The guy on Broadway."

"They think he's a failure."

"That's harsh," I say. Even though I could see my mom saying the same thing.

"They think they worked so hard to come to America," Juhi says, "that we have to work harder and make more money than they do."

"At least you don't have to work in a store," I say. "*That* sucks." Is that true? I'm not sure, but it feels good to complain.

"Wrong," Juhi says. I look at her, puzzled. But before I can ask what she means, Juhi wraps her arms around her knees and says, "You know, Karthik, you're easy to talk to." She's wearing blue nail polish on her toes, which are perfectly formed like the rest of her.

"Yeah? My sister thinks I'm annoying." I don't know why I say that, but it's the only way to respond to a compliment.

"My sister thinks I'm annoying, too. Maybe I am."

"You're not." *Because you're perfect*, I think.

"I don't know what I am. It's like there are all these different *mes*. You know what I mean?"

"Yeah. Like we're different around different people," I say. "Which is the right one?" *Am I the grocery boy?* I wonder. *The dweeb? Or the budding actor? And who is Juhi? The one in school before this summer, the one with Jacob Donnell, or the one with me now?*

"Exactly! Which is the right one?" she repeats. She smiles and my stomach does a weird thing where it drops down and goes back up. I sneak a look at her. She's looking at me, too. What does she see—a Lenny-look-alike? An Indian guy? Me?

We talk longer about what we think ninth grade will be like and what clubs we might join in high school. Juhi mentions the school musical again to me, and I nod, even though I hadn't thought of it yet, and I wouldn't want my mom giving me grief about it either, or calling me a failure. It's just nice to talk to Juhi, to hear her say my name right. I'm not Cutie or Dweeb or whatever. I'm me.

As we're talking, we hear the sound of a door opening. Juhi and I jump up.

"I found them," someone says. It's the priest who introduced the dancers onstage.

Two people appear behind him—one is my dad, the other is Juhi's mom.

"Juhi," Mrs. Shah says loudly. "Where have you been? Asha finished long time back."

"Karthik, let's go," Dad says. "Raj is in the car."

Mrs. Shah pulls on Juhi's arm and says, "Come, everyone is waiting." Then she looks at me like I'm a mushroom growing inside her home. Juhi rolls her eyes apologetically at me when her mom isn't looking. It's the most beautiful eye roll I've ever seen. So I roll my eyes back and it's like we're in on a secret.

In the car, Raj makes room for me in the back. "Karthik," he says, "did you break my bike yet with your bony butt?"

On the ride home, he keeps jabbing me with his big elbows, asking why I'm growing my hair out like a girl, or why my arms are like sticks, or if I've ever thrown a football in my life. He seems to sense that something wonderful happened to me inside the temple other than God. So he tells me disgusting stories about how some animals eat their prey whole, and how their bones get crushed or their eyeballs pop out, until I'll probably have nightmares about being swallowed alive by a python. Still, nothing Raj says can make the feeling inside me go away.

I have a list for the evening, and it's: happy, happy, happy.

Chapter 11

Raj gets to sleep in my bed, and I end up on the floor in a sleeping bag. It seems like since Raj is the guest, he should get the floor. But my parents have different ideas about guests. And Raj.

WHY HAVING MY COUSIN OVER SUCKS

- He keeps talking when you want him to shut up.
- He asks a lot of annoying questions.
- He ALWAYS knows what you're thinking.

Raj pounds my pillow down with his giant hands and settles into my bed.

"What were you doing with that girl?" he asks.

I try to bunch up the sleeping bag, but I can still feel the hard floor underneath. I don't know how Miles slept here last night.

"She's Asha Shah's sister, isn't she?" Raj continues when I don't answer.

"So?" I ask. I bunch up my paper-thin pillow, too. It's a "guest" pillow, which means it's the one no one else wants. You would think Raj would get the guest pillow, but no.

"So I know Asha from track and cross-country meets. And if Juhi's the same, she's totally out of your league, man. Like, don't even try, you'll just be a loser."

I feel my temperature rise, and I wonder if I can put up with Raj without strangling him. Of course, if it came to a strangling contest, Raj would win, being about a hundred pounds heavier than me and without a conscience. So I pretend to nod off to sleep on my guest pillow. I don't say a word, even when I hear him whispering from my bed, "Loser, loser . . ."

He gives up at last, and maybe I *am* tired, because before I know it, I do fall asleep, and I'm startled to find sunshine splashing across the top of my sleeping bag. It's early morning, maybe seven o'clock, and my neck is sore.

Last night's conversation with Juhi comes drifting back to me. I'd never talked to her so much before. I was always worried I would say something silly. Because maybe Raj is right, and she's out of my league. Still, Juhi did say I was easy to talk to. Does she find Jacob Donnell easy to talk to? I'm pretty sure that isn't why she hangs out with him—because of his talking skills. Around fifth grade, he started calling me Kar-dick. Then so did a bunch of other people. I think that's why I hate Jacob. Because he made everyone say my name wrong. And now I have to live with his pointless joke.

Raj is still asleep, so I pull Shanthi's play out of my backpack. I start from where I left off at the temple, when Lenny runs off.

SCENE 2
Bernsteins' kitchen. JENNIE makes oatmeal at the stove. SAM reads newspaper at the table.

SAM: I bet Clara didn't know what to do with that piano. That's why she sends it to us.

JENNIE: Doesn't matter. Lenny likes the piano.

LENNY: I already know "Goodnight, Sweetheart," and "When the Saints Go Marching In."

SAM: (rustles newspaper) Infernal noise. What good is a piano if none of us plays?

JENNIE: Lenny will play! Let Lenny play.

SAM: Better he studies his Latin.

JENNIE: (Ruffles Lenny's hair) When you were a little boy you couldn't say music, you could only say "moynik."

LENNY: Yeah, you tell me that a million times!

JENNIE: Here's your moynik, Lenny. Music at last!

(Scene fades to dark while spotlight shines on LENNY.)

LENNY: (to audience) I just need a chance. It's not every day a piano shows up in your apartment. In school, we learned that phrase: carpe diem. Can't I do that? Carpe diem? I'm a kid, but not for long. I'll show everyone. I'll make a name for myself.

"Where am I?" a voice asks from my bed.

"Your home away from home," I say. "Fresh sheets, scented pillowcases, guest towels."

Raj groans and rolls over. "Your bed sucks," he says. A few moments later, I hear him snoring quietly again. I keep reading.

BEING LENNY (THE PLAY) IN 5 PARTS

- Gets a piano from Aunt Clara when he's ten
- Wants to be a musician but his dad won't let him (his mom is okay)
- Lenny plays anyway, charges for lessons
- Sneaks into a church and performs "When the Saints Go Marching In" on the church organ until he's caught by the police (I think this is made up, there's nothing like that in the Bernstein book)
- Plays brilliantly at his recital and his dad says, "Lenny is brilliant, and for that I'm afraid."

When I get to that last line, I wonder, why is Lenny's dad afraid? Is that part made up, too? Even so, it gives me goose bumps. I think it's a good ending. I want to tell Shanthi that. I can't wait to see her. I can't wait to run through my lines. And I can't wait to see Juhi again.

Chapter 12

The store doesn't open until noon on Sundays, so I have the morning free. I walk up and down Comm Ave, hoping to run into Miles. I could have gone to his place, but I always feel strange being there on the weekends. Most of the time, he and his dad are throwing a football in front of their building, or else they're watching football on TV. Miles never tells me to not come over, but when I do, I feel out of place.

His dad is decent. I've never heard him say anything nasty, but he's either eating or cooking or throwing around a ball or fixing a pipe under the kitchen sink. He doesn't do the crossword or play chess. He doesn't seem to know what else to do around a brainy kid like Miles.

As I walk on Harvard, I wonder, what is braininess anyway?

- Knowing the life cycle of a honeybee or Newton's laws of thermodynamics.
- Doing things in your head: long division, word scrambles, grocery store lists.
- Understanding cause and effect, like, adding water to acid means an *explosion*.
- Knowing more than others do.

But I'm not sure that's all there is to it. Braininess has to be more than just memorizing stuff. It has to be something else, too, like knowing how to sing or how to be onstage so people want to watch you. Or knowing what to say and when to say it. That's the kind of braininess I'd like to have.

Outside, the air is surprisingly calm and quiet, so I turn up Nitya's iPod. I finished *West Side Story* and have been cycling through some of her other songs. Most of it is awful, but there's also some good stuff like the Cranberries, Green Day, and jazz by Coltrane at the Village Vanguard.

There's also this thing about listening to music outside—like how gas expands to fill a container. Music expands, too, and when you're outside, you are in that air, which surrounds you like a huge, musical bubble. *Scientists confirm the presence of a strange, mysterious music bubble floating down the streets of Allston, enveloping a fourteen-year-old boy with hair like Lenny Bernstein.*

On Harvard Ave, I have to walk around a long line of people waiting outside the House of Chaat. Then I cross the street to the Saigon Rose, where I see Binh outside the restaurant, and I put my iPod away. We talk for a little bit, then Binh says he has to go inside to get the tables ready for the lunch crowd trickling in. "I will join you later," he says. "Maybe at Carmine's."

I'm about to tell him I won't be going there anymore. Last night I decided that if I was rehearsing a play, I wouldn't have time for ice cream. But then I remember I haven't told Binh about the play. Behind me, there's honking, because people in front of House of Chaat are blocking traffic.

"It is so busy over there," Binh says. "They are racking up business. My family is envious. Worried, too. But it is okay, right?"

"It's okay," I agree. Though I don't really know. "Is their food good?"

Binh shrugs. "I have not tried. I do not know 'chaat.'"

"It's Indian food."

"Okay, we go there one day instead of ice cream," Binh says. From inside, we can hear his mom yelling at him. "Oops. Got to go. Enjoy the Caramel Swirl for me."

I check my phone and decide maybe there's time to go to Carmine's one last time before I head to the store. When I get there, who do I see at the counter—Juhi! I think, maybe she'll want to look at the script like we did last night. I still have it in my backpack. We can sit together and eat ice cream and read about Lenny. But then I do a double take as she goes back to a booth and I notice who else is there: Sara, Jacob, and Hoodie.

They all see me. Juhi looks like she isn't sure what to do. I don't know what to do either. So I stand in line behind a girl in a big, poofy skirt, who's ordering a Strawberry Daiquiri on a cone. Meanwhile, I can hear voices behind me laughing, until I'm sure there's something in the works. *Please let me get out of here with nothing happening.* Until yesterday, I'd never really talked to Juhi. Now that I have, there's more to lose. Finally, the poofy-skirt girl is gone. I'm next.

"Caramel Swirl in a bowl," I say hoarsely. What's happening to my voice? I clear my throat.

"Bowl or cone?" the boy behind the counter asks.

"A bowl," I repeat.

More laughter behind me. God, are they listening?

"That will be—"

"I know," I cut in, plunking down the money on the counter. I get my bowl of ice cream and head for the door. Then I hear a voice call out.

"Hey, Kar-dick, something fell out of your backpack."

I turn reluctantly. "No, it didn't," I say evenly.

Before I can stop him, Jacob lunges and grabs the backpack off my shoulder. "Let me check for you," he says. He sits back in the booth, where everyone is giggling.

"Give it back," I say, even though I know Jacob won't. Once, he stole my backpack in sixth grade and threw it inside the boys' bathroom. Binh was the one who found it. It was stuffed with toilet paper and wet paper towels. I had to throw out my binder full of math homework and Miles's copy of *Lord of the Rings* that he'd lent me, because they were both soaked.

"What you got in here, Kar-dick?" Jacob asks now.

"Kar-dick thinks it's still school," Sara says.

Jacob rummages through my backpack. I lean over to snatch it, but Jacob blocks me and slowly pulls out items one by one: my wallet, some baseball cards Miles gave me, a pair of old socks I'd forgotten about that makes everyone at the table go ewww.

Hoodie opens my wallet. "He's got a picture of his family!" he announces.

Since when was that a crime? Even so, I'm cursing my mom for putting it in there. Meanwhile, my Caramel Swirl is melting in my bowl.

"How much money?" Sara asks.

"Kar-dick's broke," Hoodie says, pocketing the ten dollars from my wallet.

Jacob, at last, pulls out the play.

"Gross, it's got food spilled all over it," Sara says.

"It smells bad," Hoodie says.

Jacob flips through. "It's a play, Kar-dick. What gives? *Being Lenny*." He starts reading out the lines in a high falsetto. "Nobody will believe me when I tell them, I knew about this," he shrieks.

"About what?" Hoodie asks.

"That I'm a butt-wipe," Jacob says.

I swallow. It's Shanthi's play, but it feels like they're ripping out a part of me. I search my mind for something to say, but as usual, it's: blank, blank, blank.

"Sounds boring," Juhi says. "Let's get out of here."

I stare at her. *Sounds boring?*

Everyone gets up one by one and shoves their way past me.

"Let's dump it in the trash," Sara says, lifting up the script.

"The movie starts in ten minutes," Juhi says. "We should go."

So Sara tosses the play on the floor and steps on it with her sneakers.

Jacob grins at me. "Here's your backpack," he says, and hands it over to me all nice-like.

Then the group shuffles out the door into the glaring sunlight, as I'm left with a crumpled family photo, an empty wallet, and a shoe print on Lenny.

WHAT I SHOULD HAVE SAID TO JACOB

- Next time you take my backpack, you're toast.
- Next time you say my name wrong, you're toast.
- Actually, you're already toast.
- You're the toast that's burnt and on the floor, jam side down, stepped on.

WHAT I SHOULD HAVE SAID TO JUHI

- Your friends suck.
- If Jacob is the burnt toast, then you're the jam.
- Wow, I'm really out of ideas.

Chapter 13

"Karthu, what are you doing here already?" Dad is surprised to see me at the store. Usually I don't get there until noon on Sundays. He looks at me more closely. "Are you okay?"

I feel my lips tremble and I'm mortified. When Hoodie and Jacob pulled down my pants in second grade, or tripped me in the cafeteria this year so my tray went flying and I had nothing to eat for lunch except a bag of chips, or even when they made ten Kar-dick jokes in front of the entire eighth-grade English class when Mrs. Dubois stepped out of the room, I never said anything and I never cried. But today is different. And I can't tell my dad. I can't even tell myself.

"I'm fine," I say gruffly.

"Then run over some biscuits to Mr. Jain. And two mangos to Mrs. Rodrigues."

I want to say no. I want to say forget about your store and let's move to Worcester already. But I don't. Instead, I get the deliveries ready as he goes to the back room. I can hear him talking with Aasif. Otherwise, the store is quiet and empty. As I pack the bags, the whole thing at the ice cream shop reruns in my head. Getting my money stolen. Jacob reading Shanthi's play out loud. Sara stomping on it. Juhi saying nothing.

My hand stops, the box of Parle-G biscuits in my hand. The awful feeling in me blossoms. It's bad enough Juhi saw what happened. But it's worse that she made me feel like a loser, too. Why didn't I say something? Forget the toast. Why didn't I punch Jacob in the face? Even if I've never punched anyone in my life. There's a first for everything.

When I get to Mr. Jain's, he opens the door wearing a bright blue shirt with a banana print and a pair of khaki shorts. His bare legs are white and hairless and look like toothpicks.

"Whoa, Mr. J. Do you have an off switch?" I pretend to shield my eyes from his shirt.

I don't think he'll get my joke, but he actually grins. There are faint beads of sweat along his brow. "This is the most hideous shirt I own," he says. "But it's almost brand-new, and I wanted to wear something different. I went a few rounds around the neighborhood and I feel marvelous."

I give him the biscuits, trying not to laugh. Two things that don't go together: Mr. Jain's accent and the word "marvelous."

He hands me money for the biscuits. "Do you know every day when I was a little boy in Rajasthan, we had Parle-G with tea? My mother started the pot early morning. She would boil and boil that pot until the tea leaves were so thick you could write with them. Ha! Nothing like what they make here. So weak, like piss."

"Is Sachin Tendulkar a huge tea fan?" This is the only Indian cricket player's name that I know. Since I don't have a clue about tea, I figure I'll mention him instead.

Mr. Jain's face lights up. It's like the sun rising over the sea of his blue shirt. "You know who Tendulkar is?"

"Sure," I say. Not really, but Aasif tells me stuff. "Most scores, most innings." That's what Aasif said.

"In cricket," Mr. Jain shouts, "Tendulkar is king!" He hikes up the waistline of his khaki shorts. "Now, what I was saying about my mother's tea?"

Wow, back to tea. I edge to the door. "Gotta go. More deliveries."

"That's right, you are busy busy," Mr. Jain says. "But remember, tea is life."

"Yep."

"Twice a day. And throw in a bowl of papdi chaat like what they sell around the corner."

This is new. "You mean House of Chaat?"

"Who knows? I don't bother with names. But those fellows got it right. What they make, it *tastes* like India. Much better than the frozen samosas at your store."

"Yeah? I'll have to stop by."

"Take care, Karthik, stay out of mischief." Mr. Jain chuckles and disappears into his apartment.

I step out onto the street. That's the most I've ever talked to Mr. Jain. He was happier than normal, and for some reason, I notice I'm feeling a little better, too.

At Mrs. Rodrigues's, she comes down as soon as I buzz her.

"Did you bring the mangos?" she asks in her usual way.

"Yes, two mangos, extra-ripe," I say. Then I add, "I smelled them first."

It's true. At the store, I'd paused for a moment in front of the bin. Was there a way to tell which mangos were extra-ripe without being spoiled? I always went for the soft ones, but maybe too soft was bad. So I smelled them and picked two that smelled like the ones mom slices for us at home. Who knows?

Mrs. Rodrigues looks at me, and I think I should've kept my mouth shut, that she's going to tell me, yuck, I don't want pre-smelled mangos! But she actually nods and says, "Good." She pulls them out of the bag. "See this one? It smells ripe. This other one? Not so much."

Great. I wait for her to give the non-smelly one back to me.

Instead she hands me a tip. This time it's fifty cents. "You're getting better," she says.

Then she goes back inside the elevator. What am I going to do with fifty cents? Not enough to buy ice cream. Not that I'm buying anymore. So I put the two quarters in my pocket, and they're warm against my fingers.

HOW TO ACT LIKE LENNY

- Walk tall.
- Tilt your head back and smile with your teeth showing.
- Say "it's wild!" when something's cool.
- Really like Mahler and Gershwin and the piano in general.
- Forget Jacob Donnell's face.

Chapter 14

"It's you," Shanthi says when she opens the door. She says this every time she sees me. Who does she expect? It's Monday, and I've brought her a bag of spicy chips and two Fantas, which she ordered over the phone.

She's wearing a tee and a long blue skirt with bells on it that jingle when she walks. She pays for the Fanta and chips. "You want some?"

I shake my head. I've been running deliveries all day and feel hot and gross.

She opens her bag of chips. "So, did you bring the play?"

I nod.

"Good, take it out—let's look at it."

"I, uh . . ."

"Don't be shy." She points to my backpack on the floor. So as she's eating her chips, I'm forced to pull the play out and show her all the things that happened to it. I wait for her to yell at me for damaging her only copy, and that it's all a big mistake to trust a fourteen-year-old with her work. Which is probably true. It *is* a big mistake. "Hmm," she says.

"Sorry about the, uh, way it looks."

"I'm flattered. You read my play. Look at all the food stains. And is that . . . a shoe print?"

"I dropped it," I mumble, hating myself.

Shanthi flips open the pages. "Let's start. I'll read a few lines, then you repeat after me."

"Are you sure about this?" I'm starting to get cold feet. I practiced all weekend. I even came up with tips for acting like Lenny. But ever since yesterday happened, I can only think of Jacob and Hoodie ragging on me with the same lines I have to say now in front of Shanthi. Not exactly inspiring.

"*Pretend*. Anyone can pretend."

Unless you've had your pants pulled down. I bet that never happened to Lenny.

"Maybe we should do it another time. My dad will say I'm late."

"Ten minutes. What's wrong, Karthik? I thought you were okay doing this." She searches my face and then looks at the script, and at the shoe print still there. Something seems to register, an understanding, and suddenly I don't want her to ask me.

"I'm ready," I say quickly. "It's going to be uh, wild."

Shanthi gives me a strange look. "Right. Okay, I'll read you the first line. Nobody—"

"Nobody will believe me when I tell them, I knew about this."

She looks at me.

"I know the first line."

"What about the second line?"

"Yeah, I know it, too."

She sits back. "You memorized the lines already?"

"I read the beginning a few times. And I remember."

"Okay," she says. "Let's do it."

Chapter 15

Ten minutes later.

"Say it with more feeling!"

"I just need a chance," I say wearily. I've repeated this line five times already. I've been standing tall, smiling and everything, and I thought I knew the words, but no matter how I say them, it's not right for her.

"I *just* need a chance," Shanthi says. She holds up a clenched hand in the air.

"I just need a chance," I repeat. I keep my hand down. It seems silly. This acting thing is harder than I thought.

"Don't you see, this is when Lenny decides what he wants to do with his life." Shanthi clasps her hands earnestly as she speaks. Maybe she should be Lenny, not me.

But I know what she's saying. I'm not a clod. There are plenty of things I would want to do with my life if I could. Like find a way to make Jacob Donnell's face disappear. Hoodie's, too. It would be pretty hard to make Kar-dick jokes without a face.

"Karthik, did you hear what I said?"

I nod. We go over the scene again.

"It's not what *you* want," I say. "It's what I want."

"But you don't know what you want," Shanthi says, reading Sam's part. "That's why I'm helping you, son."

I lower the script. "Do you think Lenny's dad would say it like that?"

"Why? He doesn't want Lenny wasting his time on the piano. How should he say it?"

I think about my mom. "He'd say, Lenny, you're a twit."

Shanthi shakes out the last crumbs of the spicy chips, tipping the bag to her mouth, which reminds me of Juhi eating her cone from the bottom. "Ugh, I keep thinking I'm done and then something comes up. I hate not knowing if the play is good. I hate worrying about it. I hate worrying about myself."

"Your play is good," I say. I mean it.

Shanthi smiles. "Thanks. Try telling that to my mom."

"Is that why she isn't speaking to you? Because you're writing plays?"

She looks at me curiously. "You really do remember everything, don't you? I said that, but it's not exactly true. I guess you could say I'm the one not speaking to her."

"What do you mean? Why not?"

"While I'm in this playwriting program, I'm not talking to her or my dad. They don't like what I'm doing. So I told them I wanted one year without hearing all their negative stuff."

"For real, you're not talking to them? No phone calls, even?"

"Yep," Shanthi says. "It's the only way I could get anything done. Not having their voices in my head. Plus, they're not paying. I got a scholarship. So I'm totally on my own."

Whoa. I try to imagine not talking to my parents for a year: no phone calls, no articles, no dinner conversations, no wishing me goodnight before I go to bed. A year of silence would be weird.

"Are they . . . okay with it?" I ask. My mom would flip.

Shanthi shrugs. "Sometimes we have to figure out who we are without our parents telling us."

"Like Lenny becoming a musician."

She smiles. "Yeah, like him. I mean, no one's perfect. He wasn't. But he did have his own ideas. That's what my play is about. It's about the moment when we learn to make up our own mind."

"When he got the piano, that's when Lenny did."

"Exactly. He was young. It took me until college. And I guess for others, maybe never, and how sad is that? Not having your own ideas about what you want to be."

Not having your own ideas. I don't want that. I want to be my own person. But I don't think I could handle giving my parents the silent treatment either.

Just then, my phone vibrates in my pocket. It's my dad calling me about the groceries. I ignore him. I figure that's enough silent treatment.

"So, this was a good . . . start," Shanthi says to me. "Tomorrow we'll go over the scene again."

"You think I'm okay?" I'm suddenly anxious. Hadn't we already gone over the scene sixteen times? I know—I kept track.

She hands me my script. "You will be," she says.

Will be? "So I suck now."

She picks her words carefully. "Remember, you're not Karthik. You're this other boy living in the 1930s who wants to be a musician and his dad won't let him."

"So I do suck."

"Don't worry. I really think there's something in you. Like you were meant to play Lenny."

Really? Other than the hair, I don't see a world-class musician in me.

"Maybe you should watch *West Side Story*. Or listen to something else Lenny wrote. Let his music speak to you. Get into his character."

What is she talking about? I'm starting to feel glum. I thought this acting thing would be a lot easier. I've memorized grocery lists, news articles, the periodic table, and French conjugations at school. But just memorizing my lines doesn't seem to be enough for Shanthi. Instead, she says I have to get into character. What does that even mean? I tried standing tall and throwing my head back and smiling like I saw Lenny do in his Harvard lectures. Didn't Shanthi notice that? The book she gave me certainly didn't help. Who wants to look at a bunch of pictures of Lenny at his beach house in Sharon? What do they tell me about *being* Lenny? Then I get another idea.

A few minutes later, I'm parking my bike in front of the Allston library. I know I'll be late to the store and my dad will be pissed, but if I hurry maybe it won't matter. Inside, I find the aisle quickly.

What I don't expect is how many books there are on acting: *Acting for Dummies*, *Learn to Act in 30 Days*, and a few other self-help books like *Stop Acting and Start Living*. I flip through several books and I keep seeing the same things:

HOW TO BE AN ACTOR . . .
OR NOT BE AN ACTOR

- Be real but learn to fake it.
- Memorize your lines but don't sound rehearsed.
- Go to acting school.
- Don't go to acting school.
- Know yourself.
- Know others.
- Don't quit.
- Unless you suck (which you'll know soon enough).

Yikes. It sounds so complicated, like I'm doomed before I start. I just want a simple book on getting into character. That's what Shanthi wanted, right? And something that doesn't announce to the world what I'm reading. If I walked home with a bright yellow *Acting for Dummies*, my mom would be on me like a fly on a rotten mango. So I look through the bookshelves again and finally settle on *An Actor's Tricks* by someone named Yoshi Oida. He's wearing a white robe on the cover like he's doing martial arts, not a play. Mom's always getting on my case to exercise. Hopefully she won't look at the title too carefully. Tai chi, anyone?

Chapter 16

At the store, Dad is mopping around the refrigerator. The way's he's doing it without looking at me, I must be in trouble. I brace myself.

"Are there more deliveries?" I ask. There's no one in the store except Aasif in the back.

Dad keeps mopping. A pool of water bleeds from under the refrigerators like a crime scene.

"Yes," he says finally. "And they need it right away."

I wait for him to yell at me, but he doesn't. Then at that moment, the door opens. It's a guy wearing a gray shirt with his name inside a white oval. When I see what it says, I don't believe it. Really?

"Hi there," Lenny says. "You need someone to look at your refrigerator?"

He doesn't look anything like Lenny Bernstein. Or the car mechanic Lenny who changed the oil in our Volvo last week. This Lenny has a beard, his face is round, and his hair is dirty blond. The world is teeming with Lennys.

By now, Aasif has come over from the back room to see what's going on.

"Yes, the refrigerator keeps leaking. We've tried everything," Dad says. "There are two, and they're both leaking, actually. But one is worse than the other."

"All right, let's take a look," Refrigerator Lenny says. "It's that time of the year when everything falls apart."

As I ponder over the wisdom of Refrigerator Lenny's words, Dad puts the mop away and brings me a packet marked amchur powder. "Take this to 120 Harvard Ave," he says.

"Isn't that across from Binh's restaurant? Wait, is that . . ."

"Yes," Dad says.

Behind him, Refrigerator Lenny is moving one of the refrigerators forward. He whistles. "Wow, the back of this fridge sure is clean."

Aasif and I look at each other. Well, at least I did something right with the hand vac.

Dad turns to me. "When you're there, buy one papdi chaat to go." He watches as Refrigerator Lenny pulls out a screwdriver from his toolbox.

"You talking about that new chaat place on Harvard?" Refrigerator Lenny asks. "Good stuff. But boy, that line outside is nuts."

"Hey, Mr. Jain was raving about the papdi chaat, too," I say.

"Let's see what's so special," Dad says casually.

Behind him, Aasif rolls his eyes.

I look at him, puzzled. Why does my dad care about the papdi chaat?

"Aha," Refrigerator Lenny says, popping the grill off the back of the first refrigerator. "Not so pretty after all."

His pronouncement fills the air.

"That bad?" Aasif asks.

Is it a catastrophe or a nuisance? I turn to Dad's face for clues, but it's unreadable.

Instead he waves me off. "Just bring back the papdi chaat. And don't get distracted."

Some things never change.

As I bike to House of Chaat, I think of Carmine's fifty flavors. But then I remember Jacob, Hoodie, and Sara and Juhi sitting there saying nothing. So I run through the lines to Shanthi's play instead. *It's not every day that a piano shows up in your apartment.*

Inside, it's wicked hot, with people waiting in line for their orders. Two fans are blowing around hot air and the smell of sweat and fried onions mixed together.

"Number 145," calls a guy from the counter. "Number 148. Number 147."

Wow, they move fast.

I survey the rest of the place: bright orange walls, posters of the Taj Mahal and Ganges River, swivel seats and melamine tables nailed down (like who's going to take them?). Around me, there are grad students sitting in one corner, old Indian ladies balanced on the nailed-down stools as they dip samosas into chutney, a whole family with their two kids yelling at each other, their crayons everywhere, and two policemen in uniform having coffee and potato tikka.

"Hey," someone calls out to me from the counter, "you are here to place an order? The line starts all the way back there."

"Yes," I say. "No. I mean I came to deliver the amchur powder first." He then gestures for me to come through the door in the back. Behind the doors, the kitchen is in full swing. There are people frying food at the stove, others in line, assembling plates, and I hear the guy say something in Hindi, with the words "grocery bachcha" thrown in, which I guess refers to me.

"Hey Juhi, can you pay him?" he asks before going back to the counter.

To my astonishment, at the end of the line, Juhi is packing orders inside brown paper bags. "Satish Uncle, I'm busy, we're missing something from this order, and . . ." She sees me and stops. "What are you doing here?"

"Amchur powder," I mumble.

"Oh, right." She takes the plastic packet from me. "Uh, how much?"

I tell her the amount, and she takes out a cash box from one of the drawers under the counter. "Just a sec," she says. Her super straight hair is tied up with a black net over it, and there are smudges of grease on her apron. This is the last place I'd expect to see her. "Here you go," she says, holding out the money to me.

When our eyes meet, she's completely mortified. My stomach turns. I have to get out of here.

"Thanks, gotta go. I know where the exit is." I turn around and almost run into someone coming through the swinging door.

"Karthik, wait." She follows me out the door to the customer area, where the line is still there and growing.

"I have to go. My dad needs me at the store." This makes me remember the papdi chaat Dad wanted me to bring back. Shoot. The line is too long, and there's no way I'm staying.

Juhi says to the guys at the counter, "I'm coming back, okay?"

"Beta, the orders don't pack themselves," says the guy she calls Satish Uncle, the one who brought me to the kitchen.

Juhi pulls me to the back, near the restrooms. She's twisted the ends of her apron in her hand. "So, uh, did you finish Shanthi's play?"

"Yeah."

"Was it good?"

I shrug without looking at her.

"Maybe we could get some ice cream later and read it for a while."

I pause. "So the 'boring' play sounds interesting to you now? Or maybe you thought I could buy ice cream with the money Hoodie stole from me."

She winces. "I'm sorry. They were awful to you."

"Yeah, well, you weren't any better." I can't believe I'm telling her this.

"Look, that was the only way they were going to leave you alone. And it worked. They didn't throw away the play."

"I'm *so* glad your plan worked."

"Well, I didn't hear you saying anything. Maybe you have to stand up for yourself."

I feel myself turn red. "Nothing ever works on Jacob," I mumble. "He just gets worse."

I say that, but I know she's right. I need to find a way to stand up to Jacob. But does that mean she had to go along with him?

Juhi sighs. "Jacob has always been . . . what's the word?"

"A jerk."

She flushes. "But when I'm with him, I get to . . . do things. Sara, too."

"Like what? Pull the wings off flies?"

She smiles in spite of herself. "No. I see movies with them. Jacob always pays for me, even when I tell him not to. Then last week, he took me boating with his dad on the Charles. He's really strong. He's probably going to be on crew."

I watch the line moving behind her. "They're still not nice, Juhi. You know that."

"I *always* do what my parents say," Juhi says savagely. "It's Satish Uncle's restaurant, but my parents are the managers and they're making me help out, whether I want to or not. I only get a few breaks and that's when I hang out with Jacob and Sara. They're not into all this smelly onion stuff."

"What stuff?"

Juhi points to her apron. "This. You think I want to do this? First it was just on the weekends at my dad's 7-Eleven. Then my uncle came along with this chaat place and that's what I've been doing every day this summer. Smelling like onions."

"Juhi, they're jerks! Don't you see that?" There are so many awful things Jacob has done over the years, it's impossible to make a list. Even for me. "They'll be jerks to you, too."

"I can take care of myself. Just—don't tell them, okay?"

I think of Binh, who works in his family's restaurant across the street. He doesn't care if anyone knows. "I don't talk to them anyway," I mutter.

Satish Uncle is signaling to her from the counter.

"I have to go. But I'll see you again soon. Did you start rehearsing yet?"

I nod. I hate it that she's asking to be nice. I hate it that I'm secretly glad she remembers.

"Awesome." She's about to go when she turns back to me. Black strands are coming out of her hairnet, framing her face in little wisps, and I see flour on her face. She might smell like onions, but I don't know why it matters. She's still the same person who sat in the temple and read Shanthi's play with me. "Do you want anything on the menu? It's on me."

I sigh, remembering my dad. "Fine, I guess."

It's a peace offering, but I should have said no. I should never talk to her again. Lenny wouldn't have time for people like her. He would walk out and conduct concerts around her until she went dizzy. He would tell people like Jacob to take a hike. Wasn't Lenny only twenty-five when he conducted the New York Philharmonic? Wasn't he one of the first American conductors to tour Europe? He made people listen to him, even if they didn't like who he was or where he came from. But that was him.

And I'm not Lenny.

Chapter 17

At the store, one of the refrigerators is unplugged. It's completely empty, and the lights stay off when I slide the door.

"What happened?" I ask Aasif.

"It's bust," he says. "It needs to be replaced. But we can't do that. So we transferred everything to the other fridge."

I look at the other one and it's stuffed to the brim. The frozen vegetables are mixed with the frozen entrees are mixed with the frozen snack foods and shredded coconut. You can't find anything in there. Not even a dead body. I don't know why I think that.

"So what happens?" I ask.

"You tell me," Aasif says.

"What did Refrigerator Lenny say?"

"Who?"

Dad comes out of the back room. "Don't worry about the refrigerator," he says. "We have one that's working."

"Not for long according to Refrigerator Lenny," Aasif says.

"Who?" Dad asks. "Never mind. Karthu, did you bring the stuff?"

I hold up the brown paper bag. Juhi packed it for me personally and threw in extra containers of chutney. Dad, Aasif, and I go into the back room and huddle around.

"Well, open it," Dad says.

I reach in and open the Styrofoam container on the worktable. I offer a fork to my father. He shakes his head.

"I've already tried it. You eat it. I want to see your reaction."

I glance at Aasif, who shrugs.

"I've tried it, too," he says.

What's going on? This is getting weird.

"Just eat it," Dad says. "And tell me what you think."

Reluctantly I take a bite and swallow. Wow. It's good. It's more than good. It's mouthwateringly delicious, better than anything my mom ever made. But a sudden sense of self-preservation tells me to keep quiet. It doesn't matter. My dad sees my face and his brain leaps forward.

"It's great, isn't it? You'd go back for more, wouldn't you?"

"I don't like chaat," I say carefully, "as much as I like ice cream."

It's the truth, but it isn't a truth that helps him. He lets his face relax momentarily into an expression of unhappiness I've never seen before.

Just then, we see a customer peering at us from the register. She is ready to pay. Immediately Dad wipes his face clear of everything but his Grocery Smile.

"Here we go," Aasif says under his breath.

Meanwhile, Dad strides to the register. "Mrs. Sharma, be right with you!" he calls out. On his way over, he shoves the container of papdi chaat into the trash before anyone can have a second bite.

I can't remember who said it first, my mother or Nitya. But we all agree. What is the big deal with House of Chaat? But my dad insists on stewing over it all through dinner.

"Chaat is an easy sell," he says. "Everyone has time for a spicy snack."

My mother ladles curry onto my plate skeptically. "Everyone does *not* have time for a spicy snack. I've got laundry to do. And grocery shopping. Cutie, stop whistling."

"That's because we don't spend a dime eating out," Dad says. "Karthik, did you hear your mother?"

"He just permanently makes noise," Nitya says.

It's a *song*. Why doesn't anyone hear that?

"Other people," Dad continues, "spend money on food and they like to snack."

"Snack?" Mom repeats. "I thought they liked BMWs."

"Not now," Dad insists. "They can only afford small luxuries. Like manicures and spicy snacks."

Nitya bursts out laughing. Dad gives her an evil, evil look.

"I'm sorry," she says. "Manicures and spicy snacks?"

"Maybe it's the economy," I venture.

"Right, Birdbrain," Nitya says. "People are losing their homes and buying spicy snacks."

"Don't call him Birdbrain," Mom says.

"But calling me Baby is okay. Way to traumatize me forever."

"Cutie, did you read the article I left for you?" Mom asks me. By "left for you," she means taping it to my door with a big "Read this!!" scrawled across the top in Sharpie.

"Yeah," I say. "About robo dogs."

"Not everyone has time for grocery shopping," Dad goes on.

"Well, isn't that why you have deliveries, Manjesh?" Mom asks. "Cutie, this veterinarian prosthetics is a whole new field. That's what the article said. Dogs getting artificial limbs just like people. Now they can run and walk and play catch again."

"Maybe people don't want to cook anymore," Dad says darkly.

"Do you know how much veterinary prosthetic surgeons make?" Mom says. It's amazing how she and my dad can be talking about two different things at the same time.

"You want the Dweeb to be a dog surgeon?" Nitya asks. "He can't even use a knife and fork properly."

"Well, you kids always liked dogs," Mom says.

"To play with!" Nitya says. "Not to operate on."

"Dog surgery," Dad says. "Really? That's more important than what I'm saying."

Mom sighs. "Of course not. Go on, what were you saying?"

"It's not about the deliveries," Dad says quietly. "It's about people changing. You can't sell basmati rice to someone who wants potato tiki in a Styrofoam box."

There is a silence as we try to make sense of what my dad is saying.

"You mean you should be selling chaat instead of groceries?" Nitya asks blankly.

Dad doesn't answer. Instead he shoves a large wedge of roti and curry into his mouth. "It's like Ferdinand all over."

"Oh, not Ferdinand." My mom sighs again.

"Ferdinand?" I ask. "Like the bull?" The only Ferdinand I know is the one I read about when I was little.

"No, Ferdinand Delgado, from your father's old job," Mom explains.

"Never mind," my dad says, all surly. "Finish your roti. No talking anyone."

Pleasant meal it's turning out to be.

My sister finishes her bird-size portion and gets up from the table, leaving me alone with my parents and the ghost of Ferdinand, whoever he is.

"You're overreacting," Mom says. "Groceries and chaat are two different things."

"You'll see," Dad says. "This place, if it's good, will draw people. Away from us."

Is that what this is about? House of Chaat stealing our customers? I suddenly remember that comment Mr. Jain made about frozen samosas not being as good. Was he lured away by a bowl of papdi chaat?

"How can a restaurant do anything to a grocery store?" I ask. "Anyway, they're always ordering ingredients from us. They need us."

"It's that Satish Shah," Dad says bitterly. "He was a snake in the grass in Queens when he was in the grocery business."

I swallow my food. "You know him?" I ask slowly.

"He was my distributor," Dad says. "Until he moved here. Runs that chaat shop with his brother."

Juhi's dad. My dad is talking about Juhi's family. I realize what Dad is actually saying. If the store goes under, he thinks Juhi's family is to blame. *They're* the ones putting us out of business.

"Well, quit," Mom says. "I've been telling you all along. Contact Pavan. There's still time to interview."

I look from my mom's face to my dad's. I don't want Dad to contact Pavan Uncle. I don't want to move to Worcester. But if the store fails, what will happen to us?

"It will pass," Dad says. "We just have to ride it out."

But we can see it in his face. He isn't sure, and neither are we.

REVISED *WEST SIDE STORY* IN 3 PARTS

- My dad owns a grocery store (Jets).
- Juhi's family owns a restaurant (Sharks).
- The Sharks eat the Jets. End of story.

Chapter 18

It's bad enough Juhi is wrecking my life. Now her family is wrecking my family, too.

In the computer room, there's a box of old movies, including *West Side Story*, which Nitya got for her birthday. She used to watch it all the time, but now she doesn't have time for movies or us. Instead, she's on her bed with her practice SAT tests spread around her.

I pop the DVD into the computer and sit back on the futon couch. As the movie begins, I hear Bernstein's opening song, the same one Shanthi played for me the first day in her apartment. I already know the whole story. I know Tony's going to fall in love with Maria, I know he's going to kill her brother, and I know he's going to get killed at the end. I know all of this, but watching the movie is different. I'm still interested and wondering what will happen next. When I get to the end, Tony dying is a lot sadder than I thought it would be. That surprises me, too. When the movie finishes, I check the credits to see who the actor playing Tony is, and his name is Richard Beymer. He did such a great job. He could act and sing *and* dance. Did he learn all that when he was young? Did he go to acting school? He sings my favorite song, "Something's Coming," and when he does, it gives me the chills, just like that line from Shanthi's play, *I knew about this.* I have to look Richard up.

I'm still watching the credits when my mom shows up.

"What were you watching?" she asks from the door, her knitting bag on her shoulder.

I look up from the screen. "Nothing. *West Side Story.*"

She pads into the room. "The Sharks and the Jets."

"I thought you never saw it."

"Wrong," she says, sitting down next to me.

When she says that, it's like a weird echo of Juhi at the temple when I said she didn't have to work in a store. I didn't understand what Juhi had meant then. Now I do.

"This movie came on the TV all the time when Daddy and I first came to Albuquerque."

"So you're a fan."

"Not really," she says. "But I remember the Sharks and the Jets. Gangs singing and dancing. Not anything like a real gang, but okay." She pulls out her needles.

"What are you making?" Every time she sits down, she's knitting.

"A shawl for Baby." She stops and shows me what she's done so far. The yarn is tiny and knit tightly together into a series of geometric shapes and patterns in different colors.

"How do you know you're not making a mistake? Where did you get the design?"

"I made it up myself," she says. "I just keep track of everything in my head. You see, you're not the only one with a memory." She goes on clicking her needles.

I think about the knitting projects in the apartment. There's even a doily thing under the computer monitor. "Do you ever make anything for Dad?"

She snorts. "What he needs is peace of mind. But there is no pattern for that."

I remember the conversation from dinner. "Who's Ferdinand?"

"Ferdinand?"

"You know, the guy in Albuquerque. The one you said, 'Not Ferdinand again.'"

My mom's needles click rapidly. "You really want to know?"

"Yeah."

"Ferdinand Delgado." More clicks of her needles. "Both he and Daddy were programmers in the same division. They were hired at the same time, put onto projects at the same time. They were set to start on the same day, then your father was delayed by a week."

"What happened?"

"You were born a month early. So Daddy started work a week later and they assigned the project he was supposed to get to Ferdinand. Daddy and Ferdinand were switched. And that's the way it went, for several years. One project became successful, the other one didn't. One project needed a new manager after four years—that became Ferdinand. The other project was shut down."

"They didn't need a manager?" I ask.

"They were 'downsized.' You know what that word means?"

"Getting fired."

"Your father felt like Ferdinand stole his job. Not on purpose, but by being in the right place at the right time."

"But I was the one born early. He should blame me."

"Yes, that would make more sense," Mom says.

"Thanks," I say. Great, I'm the reason my dad got fired.

"I'm just saying your father's reasoning isn't sensible when it comes to Ferdinand. Something changed in him. Then his brother, Pavan Uncle, invited him to Boston. Said there were computer jobs and he could get him one in his company. But Daddy had enough with computer jobs. We came, and we opened the grocery store instead. Now, seeing that chaat shop having success while he's struggling, I guess it's touching a nerve for Daddy. He's seeing someone else being in the right place at the right time, and not him. It brings back old memories of Ferdinand."

It's hard to believe that someone named Ferdinand could wreak havoc in my dad's life. I think of the story I know, about a bull named Ferdinand who would rather smell flowers than be in bullfights.

"Did Dad know how to run a store?"

"Not a single darn thing."

I notice the waver in her voice. Was it a waver of pride? Or exasperation? I listen to her needles. *Glossy hair, short waist, knitting.* Is my mom happy? She's the kind of person who knows things. Like the periodic table, or how to convert ounces to grams, or the distance from the Earth to the sun.

"Do you still wish you were a doctor?" I ask.

She looks up from her knitting. "Why?"

"Didn't you want to be one in India?"

She unrolls the yarn next to her. "Did you know the heart pumps two thousand gallons of blood a day?"

I flinch. I'm sorry, but the idea of a huge muscle pumping blood inside me freaks me out.

"Why do you make that face?" Mom asks.

I wait a moment. Then I say it. "I hate blood."

"Huh."

"Blood's gross. That's what Nitya says."

"She's a twit. I say that with love and devotion. But she doesn't know."

"How come she can say it and I can't?"

Mom stops knitting. "Blood is life. Why else do you think I want you to be a doctor?"

"So I can make lots of money."

Mom shakes her head. "My goodness, I'd tell you to go to Wall Street. Actually, don't go to Wall Street. A bunch of crooks."

I sigh.

"Of course, getting a good job is priority one," she says. "But also, being a doctor is the greatest thing." She counts her stitches for a few moments. "And understanding how we get better. Nitya can have her law. You, Cutie, look after the body. It will serve you well."

"I guess." When I was eight, Nitya fell from the slide in the playground and scraped her knee so bad there was blood everywhere, on her dress, her sock, the sidewalk. All that blood made me faint, so then Mom had to take *me* to the doctor, not Nitya (she got a Snoopy Band-Aid and was fine). "Maybe I'm not doctor material," I say.

"You're thinking about the playground, aren't you? Baby was fine! Me, I wanted to be a heart doctor. But you could choose something else. You could study the skin. Or legs. I don't know."

Legs? I don't know whether to laugh or not. Still, the other thing she just said surprises me. "You wanted to be a heart doctor?" That would explain all the gruesome articles on open-heart surgery.

"Not anymore. No chance now." She holds up her work to see what she's done.

"What do you mean? You're always saying to go after things. You could, too."

Mom goes back to knitting. "Nope, Cutie, too late for me."

"But you're telling Dad to interview. It's not too late for him. Why is it too late for you?"

She stops her needles again. When she speaks, there's a catch in her voice. "Your daddy is trying for something he already knows. He programmed for years. He studied. That's not the case for me."

I try to say how it's not true and she knows a lot of stuff, too, but she tut-tuts me and I stop. In the living room, we can hear Dad snoring on the couch.

I reach to eject the DVD from the computer when she stops me.

"I wouldn't mind watching the Sharks and the Jets."

So I restart *West Side Story*. We see the opening again with the intro song.

"This is that one by Leonard Bernstein," Mom says, her needles clicking once more. "You and Baby were talking about him."

"Yeah, he wrote the music," I say casually, not looking up from the screen.

"And you have that book, too. I found it under your bed," she says.

My stomach drops. "You were looking under my bed?" That's where I kept Shanthi's script, too. Shoot. I needed to find a better place.

"I was changing the sheets. My foot kicked the book. Not a good place to put a book."

I wait for her to ask about the script. Luckily the Yoshi Oida book is still in my backpack.

"Glad you're reading from the library," she says. I guess she assumes I got it from the library. Fine with me. "I read the intro to that Bernstein book," she goes on.

"Yeah?" I ask. I'm still waiting for some kind of interrogation.

"Yes. He's interesting."

"He was the youngest conductor of the New York Philharmonic ever," I tell her. "And he went to Harvard. He was a genius." For some reason, I want my mom to approve of Lenny. I don't want her to think like Lenny's dad did, that music isn't important. What if Lenny had listened to him and gone into the hair and beauty supply business? That would have been the worst decision in the world. There would be no *West Side Story*.

"I like he is a son of immigrants," Mom says. "See, immigrant families are hardworking, they make a name for themselves. Though I don't know, music is a tough profession. Maybe you need to have the genes for it. Anyway, don't get an overdue at the library, Cutie."

For a moment I think how I could tell her about the play. It would be so easy: *Hey Mom, you know when Leonard Bernstein was around my age, he got a piano? It started his whole music career. A piano! So there's this girl, Shanthi, who's written this play and . . .*

But I keep quiet. I don't want to hear her opinion about Lenny or Shanthi or what I should be doing with my time. Besides, the Jets have started dancing, so my mom and I stop talking and watch them instead. There's seven of them, with Riff in the lead, their arms and legs rising and falling together in unison. I need to look up who Riff is, too. All of them. What did they do? How did they get here? As I watch this time, I imagine it's *me* and I feel my insides fluttering like I'm a bird. But I'm not a bird. I'm here with my mom, and I'm not sure I will ever fly.

Chapter 19

That night I dream I'm in *West Side Story* and my dad is a Jet, but for some reason, he looks like a sheep. Not only that, Satish Shah is in my dream, too. He's laughing and grilling food in a big wok, and there are long lines of people cheering for him while Dad bleats at me, *You can never talk to Juhi, she's a Shark!* Everyone is laughing at my sheep dad, including Juhi. I wake up in a sweat.

The next morning, Miles has gone to a dental appointment, and I'm alone in the store. So in between deliveries, I try to read the book from the library, the one by Yoshi Oida. It's kind of a strange book. There aren't any acting lessons or tips. It's more like breathing exercises and how to hold your body onstage. Maybe it *is* about martial arts.

At Mrs. Rodrigues's, I buzz and she comes down and says, "You brought the mangos?" like she always does. But this time she adds, "You smelled them?"

"Yeah, they smell ripe. Like the beach." Which isn't true. When I picked the right mangos from the bin, it's like they sang to me. But I'm not telling Mrs. Rodrigues *that*.

"Like the beach," she repeats. She looks pleased.

"Uh, enjoy eating them, I guess," I say, turning to go. I don't care about the tip.

"Oh, I don't eat these," she says. "They're for my mother-in-law. Every morning she has to have them for her mango lassi. You know what that is?"

"Sure, that drink. Like a milkshake."

"Yes, and she's picky. Too ripe, it tastes spoiled. Too raw, it's scratchy. If she doesn't like it, she dumps it out in the sink."

"Wow."

She looks at me for a moment. "You have time? You want to try some?"

Mrs. Rodrigues is offering me mango lassi? Like she's being nice? She sees me hesitate.

"Never mind," she says gruffly. "You kids, you're busy, and you probably like Coke."

"Actually, I don't mind," I say, not wanting to hurt her feelings. So I ride up the elevator with her to the third floor. She opens the door, and her apartment is big and bright with all these large tropical prints on the sofas and curtains. The rug in the living room is a startling shade of turquoise, and in a corner there's a bird cage with a large parrot the same color as the rug. Next to the cage is an elderly lady in a chair with a walker next to her.

"My mother-in-law," Mrs. Rodrigues says, introducing us. Then to her in a louder voice, "This is the boy who brings the mangos. What's your name?" she asks me.

For a second I'm surprised she doesn't know. Then I realize I've never told her, so I do.

"It's Karthik who delivers," she tells her mother-in-law. "I'll go make the lassi. You stay here," Mrs. Rodrigues says to me. "Don't worry, it will only take a minute."

After she leaves, I stand there feeling awkward. Mrs. Rodrigues's mother smiles a huge, toothy smile at me. Her teeth are crooked, and she has a sharp nose and very large ears. But the rest of her is small and gray. Her hair fans out like feathers, and I realize she resembles the parrot next to her. "Is that your bird?" I ask the mother-in-law. It's the only thing I can think of to say.

She nods, still grinning. "Her name is Rani. It means princess, no? She is my life companion."

"That's nice," I say politely.

She keeps smiling and nodding at me. "The mangos you bring, they are just awful, nothing like what you get in India."

"Really?" I guess she and Mrs. Rodrigues have really high standards for fruit. I want to leave, but then Mrs. Rodrigues comes out with the mango lassi.

"Wow, this is pretty good," I say. It actually is. I drink some more.

"She is a good cook," the mother-in-law says, beaming. "And you are a good boy."

The parrot shrieks loudly and I jump.

"See, Rani agrees," says the mother-in-law, and everyone laughs, including me.

When I'm done, Mrs. Rodrigues accompanies me to the elevator.

"Thank you, Karthik," she says. "You delivered more than mangos today."

The way she says that, I feel suddenly happy. In my hand, she gives me a dollar.

Outside, it's started to rain. Big drops splash on my head and shoulders, and when they drum against the awnings over shop windows on Comm Ave, they sound like music. I start singing under my breath "Something's Coming" and I swear, the rain fits right in, like a background beat.

By the time I get to Harvard Ave, I'm drenched. Binh sees me and waves me inside. He hands me a towel that he magically has and I use it to mop up my face.

"Can I stay until it stops?" I ask him.

"Sure. Just catching up on the work." Binh points to a table where his workbook is opened. Next to it is a drawing of a boy on a motorcycle. He sees me looking at that. "Not drawing! I mean, my ESL class. It's what you say? Boring me to death. So I take breaks. Come, you want noodles?"

BINH'S RESTAURANT IN 4 PARTS

- Crowded, sometimes
- Fake flowers in pots
- Fish tanks with seahorses (yes, seahorses!)
- Good vibes (like Binh)

It's still raining hard outside as I slurp on my noodles and Binh writes in his workbook. If there's anything I love here, it's the pho. The warmth of the broth fills my stomach. My shirt is damp, and so are my shorts, but I don't mind so much with the soup inside me.

"How long do you have to do ESL?" I ask. "I thought you only did it at school."

"This is not through school. It is through library, for free. If I take now, maybe then nothing during school year. Too many other classes then, and I not have time."

I listen as Binh describes his class, how most of the students are adults who came to the US in the past year or so. Lots of Chinese people and Russians, and a few from Portugal. The class would be perfect for his mom, Binh says, but she never comes, because she doesn't want to talk in front of other people, even though her English isn't bad.

"She is too shy," Binh says. "This one Russian lady, Eva, she is not. Eva talks too much, complains too much."

I tell him about Lenny's family, how they were also Russian immigrants, but Lenny grew up here and learned music.

Binh seems interested. "Most places in the world," he says, "you could not grow up to be musician if your father is . . . What did his dad do?"

"Cosmetics."

"Really? Okay—even that. You could not grow up to be a musician if your father sells . . ."

"Wigs," I say.

We giggle.

"But in America," Binh says, "you can do that. In America, you can do anything you want. Like what if someday I want to be a comic book artist? Here it is possible. All is possible."

I like that. All is possible.

There's someone at the door. "Are you guys open yet?"

It's Sara Rimsky. She's stepped inside, carrying an umbrella and wearing a raincoat, with water dripping off her sleeves. She sees me but pretends she doesn't by Not-Saying-Hi. Instead, her attention is on Binh, and she's giving him quick, furtive looks.

He shakes his head. "Hi, Sara. No, not yet. Come back at twelve."

Her glasses are fogging up, so Binh brings her a soft napkin. He always seems to have the right thing for people. I guess it's one of his talents.

"Thanks," she says. She clumsily takes the napkin from him and dries her lenses. Without her glasses, she seems softer and rounder. For a moment, she looks like a different person.

She and Binh talk for a few more minutes. About some movie they saw. For a moment, I wonder if they saw it together. But that would be weird. Binh doesn't like Sara as far as I know. And Sara isn't even a person. More like an alien with human features who's missing a heart and brain.

"Okay, gotta run," she says to Binh. "I guess the rain is really awful, huh."

Binh smiles and says back, "Yeah, awful!" Then they smiley-smile at each other and she's gone.

"Speaking of awful," I say to him when he returns, "the rain better hide."

Binh blushes. "Oh, hide from Sara, you mean. She is not . . . so bad."

"Yes, she is!"

"No, she is . . . hard on the outside, soft on the inside. Like a boiled egg."

"I bet she'd love to hear that. I'll tell her—Binh thinks you're a boiled egg."

"Please, no. She will . . ." Binh tries to think of the right phrase.

"Kill you?"

"Sara wants to be with popular boys," he says, "and they are no good."

"No kidding."

"With them, it just takes one bad egg."

"You're really into eggs, Binh," I say.

He laughs. But there is something different about that laugh. He stops, but he still seems to be laughing. I try to figure out what it is, then from the kitchen, his mother comes over to chew him out in Vietnamese. It's the usual mom thing, and even if it's in another language, I get the gist.

Binh says to me, "Enough egg talk." He puts away his motorcycle drawing under his workbook. Then he continues his English sheets while I eat my pho. I think again about what Binh said, and I wonder who is the bad egg: Jacob, Sara, or Juhi?

HOW TO BE SUCCESSFUL (REVISED)

- Don't be a bad egg.
- Get lucky breaks. Lenny did when he got to conduct the NY Phil. So did Ferdinand when he stole my dad's job.
- Keep making a plan. This one's still hard.
- Trust your gut, which is different from making a list.

Chapter 20

The next few weeks fall into a routine. Two mangos for Mrs. Rodrigues and a cup of lassi for me, the crossword with Miles at the store, then morning and afternoon deliveries. At the beginning of the summer, there were a lot more, but these days, many of our customers have fallen off. I don't know what Dad thinks of that. He checks the remaining refrigerator every day for leaks, but so far nothing. The broken one got hauled away and there's a gap and a large water stain on the ground where it used to be.

Meanwhile, at the House of Chaat, I see something else that wasn't there before: two shiny new bicycles parked in front. Delivery bikes. There's a sign, too: WE DELIVER FOR FREE!

"They're lawless," Binh tells me. "They bike the wrong way on one-way streets. They hog up the sidewalk." Binh always wears his helmet when he rides his bicycle. He doesn't like it when people don't follow rules, especially on the street.

Lawless or not, the line outside the House of Chaat is only getting longer. There are all kinds of people waiting in line, from students to old ladies to men in suits. I even saw a Buddhist monk dressed in an orange tunic. That's something we've never seen in the grocery store. I wonder if it's a bad sign.

"Are you going to wear something special for the performance?" Juhi asks me one day when I stop by to deliver an order.

Usually we talk when she sees me at her restaurant. They're always running out of some ingredient and ordering it from the store.

"Just regular clothes, I guess," I say. What did Lenny even wear? Coat? Tie? Penny loafers? Those awful shorts that come to your knees?

"You have to get the hair right. Like with gel." She reaches to scrunch the front. This is the second time she's touched my hair. I read somewhere that if a girl touches your hair, it either means she likes you, or she thinks you need a haircut. So which one is it?

I see one of the cooks squint his eyes at me, but that might be because of the smoke from the hot oil.

By now, Juhi's uncle has tracked her down. "Juhi, hurry up, we don't have all day. We're behind on the pakoras."

"I can fry," Juhi says immediately. In spite of hating everything about working in the restaurant, she loves to cook. She says she doesn't follow recipes. She just does her own thing.

"No, beta, too much oil here, it's dangerous," Satish Shah says. He points to Juhi's bun. "Too much beautiful hair on your head."

"I can handle it, Satish Uncle," she says impatiently, but he waves her off.

"Karthik, beta. How is your father doing?" he asks me.

"Uh, he's fine," I say politely. I'm distracted by Juhi glaring at her uncle behind him.

"Tell him I say hi. I used to be a grocery distributor. Your father used to buy from me."

"Really?" I say, as if I didn't know already.

"Really, really. But now that I'm here, the restaurant business is so much better than groceries!" Satish Shah lets out a boisterous laugh.

Maybe that's why my dad hates your guts, I think.

♪

That night I wait until everyone has gone to bed, then I sneak my Bernstein book into the bathroom and prop it up on the counter, opened to a page of Lenny when he's still young. From under the sink, I pull out some hair gel that I'd bought earlier from CVS and hid behind a stack of toilet paper rolls.

I'm supposed to wet my hair first, so I do that in the sink and use a bath towel to dry my hair. Then I squeeze out a quarter-size glob of gel onto my hands and rub my palms together. Yuck. I don't like the way it feels, and also it smells kind of like Nitya and all her goopy hair products.

I look at my reflection in the mirror and try to imagine I'm Lenny doing this every morning before he took the T to Boston Latin School. The thing is I don't even know if he did that. Wear hair gel, that is. Also, this photo I'm using is when he's a little older, when he's conducting, but I still like it. He almost looks like a Jet, although he's wearing a sweater over a dress shirt. So maybe not a street gang member. More like a rebellious Harvard grad. Okay, whatever.

I apply the gel through my hair, smoothing it back and then tousling the top, like Lenny's hair. I keep working and working the gel and survey the results.

I look *nothing* like Lenny. I don't look like myself either. I'm somebody else. My face seems more angled, my eyebrows darker over my suddenly large eyes.

Well, this hair gel is useless.

I scrub it out over the sink. As I'm finishing up, there's a knock on the door. It's Nitya, so I stuff the hair gel back behind the toilet paper rolls, along with my book.

"What's taking you so long?" she asks. "I need to use the bathroom."

I open the door. "Don't fall in," I say.

She gives me a suspicious look and sniffs at me. "Why is your hair damp? Why is there water all over the sink?" She inspects my face. "Oh my god, were you trying to shave?"

I reach up to feel my jaw. "Nah. Though maybe you should."

I jump out of the way before she smacks me.

♪

The next afternoon when we're rehearsing, I mention to Shanthi what Juhi said.

"Hair gel," Shanthi repeats. "Who said that?"

"No one," I mumble. "This girl named Juhi."

Shanthi grins. "Don't worry, we'll doll you up for the performance."

"Great," I say, embarrassed. Maybe it's time to stop thinking about my hair.

Our rehearsals are part of my routine, too. Every afternoon Shanthi orders two bottles of Fanta and a bag of chips. "We're not a vending machine," Dad grumbles to me, but I don't say anything. When I deliver them to her, we go over my lines. So far we've run through the whole play, which is twenty-one minutes total, and now we're going through each scene slowly.

Shanthi says I'm getting better, but I don't think so. I don't think I'm getting into Lenny's character. I don't think I'm breathing the way Yoshi Oida says. The only thing I've done is memorize, but that seems to be the easy part.

"This is a big moment," she tells me, pointing to a scene midway in the script. "Lenny's teacher is wondering who will play the Grieg piano concerto at her recital. And Lenny says . . ."

"That will be me," I finish. "I know the line already."

"Yeah, but it's not just a line. It's a turning point. You've got to find a way to show that."

Also, near the end of the play, the stage directions say *Lenny sits at the piano and plays the Grieg piano concerto brilliantly*. Does anyone see a problem here?

Shanthi isn't fazed. "You don't need to know how to play the piano. You just fake play."

Fake play? We listen to the Grieg piano concerto on her CD player while I do that fake playing thing. Or at least I try.

"Quit laughing!" she exclaims. "This is one of the greatest piano pieces ever written."

"Sorry," I whimper, trying not to laugh.

"Let's do it again." Shanthi starts the recording while I bring my hands down in a fake pound: CHORD! CHORD-CHORD CHORD! I burst out laughing.

Shanthi is dismayed. "You need to watch Lenny on YouTube. See how he does it."

So I go home and look up Lenny videos. There are ones of him playing Mozart and Irving Berlin and someone named Shostakovich, whose name I like saying.

"Not so big," Shanthi says the next time. "Less comical. You're not Bugs Bunny."

"Hey," I say. I thought I was being just like Lenny in Vienna playing Beethoven's First Piano Concerto. Maybe Shanthi should watch that video. I saw it twenty-seven times.

PIANO TIPS IN 6 PARTS

- Relax your hands.
- Don't rush.
- Start with the right hand, then move to the left.
- Don't forget your thumb.
- Memorize.
- Practice!

I watch more videos. I watch other people, too, like Glenn Gould performing a Rachmaninoff concerto and Thelonius Monk playing jazz live in Berlin. I practice in front of the mirror in the bathroom. I practice on the coffee table in the living room.

"What the hell are you doing?" Nitya asks, her face covered in goop. She's going out somewhere with her friend on a rare night when she isn't studying.

"Have you heard of Grieg?" I ask.

"Who cares? Just stop shaking the table. I'm doing my nails."

At night I read more Yoshi Oida. It is filled with things about purification and breathing and the center line of your body. I start to wonder why I got this book instead of *Acting for Dummies*. I'm not trying to be a martial arts master. I just want to know how I can be more like Lenny. Then I get to Yoshi's section on props. He says they help actors because the audience can see the prop. The prop is used to tell the story. When I read that, something starts to click. The piano is the prop. It's the thing the audience sees. Maybe that's what Yoshi is getting at. If Lenny is happy or upset or talented, then I will have to show that with the piano. I watch more Lenny videos, but now I'm not just watching how he plays, I'm watching how he looks, too.

Mom is less enthused. "Quit watching YouTube," she scolds me. "Set the table for dinner."

But Shanthi finally notices the difference. "Hey—nice job! You *look* like you're playing!"

I grin. I don't know why it matters so much to me.

One day after rehearsing she says, "You have some time, right?"

On her wall, the clock says noon. My dad usually gives me an hour for lunch. Which means I have thirty-three minutes left. "Yeah, why?"

"There's one more thing left for you to do."

She won't tell me anything more. Surprised, I follow her outside, where we walk my bike to the corner of Comm Ave and Harvard and lock it there.

"Where are we going? It won't take too long, will it?"

Shanthi just smiles. Around the bend, the T pulls up and stops in front of us. "Come on," she says, and we climb aboard.

Chapter 21

Ten minutes later, Shanthi and I are standing in the plaza in the middle of BU campus.

"This is it?" I ask. "This is where we're going?"

There's a small crowd gathered around a sculpture called *Free at Last*, which is made up of fifty metal doves flying in honor of Martin Luther King Jr., who went to Boston University. But the crowd is not there to look at the birds.

There's another group of people there. Shanthi seems to know who they are. We go over to them and everybody is like, "Shanthi!"

She nudges me. "This is him!" she announces.

There's a guy in glasses, a girl with a nose ring and a spiky haircut, and a girl wearing a skirt with concentric patterns. The girl with the skirt says, "Oooh! He's totally Lenny!"

Everyone agrees. There are murmurs of approval.

Meanwhile, I'm totally baffled. Who are these people?

"Dudes, who brought the costumes?" asks the girl with the spiky haircut.

The guy in glasses has them. From a large bag he distributes clothes to the rest of the group.

"Okay, we'll be here rooting for you," Shanthi says. "Come Karthik, they need to get ready."

"Ready for what?"

She points to a sign someone has propped up against the metal sculpture:

BU PRESENTS: NOON DAY—FIVE-MINUTE PLAY!

"They do this every summer for one week," Shanthi explains. We stand to the side, where a small crowd of students, tourists, and faculty are waiting. "Some of them are in my playwriting program, like Eunice, that girl in the skirt. Some of them are in drama. I've been telling them about my thesis. Amanda—you know that girl with the tall hair? She's the one who said I should find someone young to play Lenny."

I look at Amanda (*nose ring, spiky hair*), who is now wearing a sundress and has tied a scarf around her spiky hair.

"Every day at noon they perform a different play," Shanthi says, "shortened down to five minutes. Monday they did *Hamlet*. Yesterday was *A Streetcar Named Desire*." We watch the group do each other's makeup. It's hard to tell what they are dressing up as.

"One of the reasons people stop by," Shanthi says, "is they pick someone from the audience to read one of the parts."

"Really? Like someone they don't know?"

"Yep. The plays always seem to work better that way. Know what I mean?"

"Yeah," I say, even though it sounds like chaos. Or something a tourist would do.

Amanda is ready and standing in front. She's wearing lipstick and heels along with her sundress and scarf, and she reminds me of someone from the 1950s. "Gentle people," she calls out to the crowd. "Welcome to Noon Day Five-Minute Plays! Where you see the world's greatest plays performed in under five minutes! Not only that, one lucky member from the audience will get a chance to perform!"

The cast looks at me. Then Amanda says, "And today's performance is a retelling of that classic tragic story we all know and love, *Romeo and Juliet.* That's right, we're doing *West Side Story.*"

Now I look at Shanthi, who shrugs demurely. "Who knew?" she murmurs.

Next, Amanda asks, "Can I have a volunteer for Tony?"

Shanthi pushes me forward and Amanda feigns surprise. "Look, gentle people. We have a young volunteer!"

"It will be good for you," Shanthi whispers to me.

The funny thing is even though I pretend I don't want to—*No! Not me! I'll suck!*—I'm kind of excited. It occurs to me I could bomb right here in front of MLK's birds and this crowd. But then I don't care.

Amanda shoves a page of lines in my hand. It's literally half a page. "Good luck, Lenny!" she says to me. She turns back to the group. "Okay, places everyone!"

She starts us off with a short monologue. Then it's me and this guy wearing glasses who's Riff, Tony's best friend.

"Hey, I think something really cool is happening soon," I read from the page.

(Like hello, he's about to meet Maria!)

The guy in the glasses tells me how it's either us or them, and that there's going to be a big fight.

Then we pretend we're at a dance as Amanda, who's Maria, dances in her sundress. Eunice, the girl with the skirt, dances, too (though I'm not sure who she's supposed to be). I step up to Amanda and we do this dance thing until Maria's brother stands between us.

"Stay away from her," he says, a scarf around his neck. (He's actually the same guy in the glasses—I guess he plays both Riff and the brother.)

As we keep reading our lines, it makes me think of last year when we read *Romeo and Juliet* in English class. The words are different, but the story is the same: young people trying to get together and society keeping them apart. Or annoying parents controlling their kids with their opinions (hmm, where have I seen this before?).

There are a few set changes but they're simple, like Eunice carrying a piece of cardboard that says "Night" across the plaza. Or when we get to the marriage scene, Amanda wearing a veil on her head and we get married by shaking hands, which makes the audience laugh. I guess the point isn't to do a play but to remind everyone that this is a story we all know.

During the last scene, we all get plastic knives and dance around the plaza with them, pretending to fight. Even some people from the audience are given plastic knives, which they wave in the air. At one point, Riff gets killed by Maria's brother, then I kill him. As he pretends to die, he gets really dramatic, yelling out "I'm dead!" before collapsing to the ground.

When it's my turn to be killed, I say, "Bye!" And then I fall down dead, too.

This time the audience laughs unsurely. Is this funny or not? But they are interested and watching. I'm lying on the ground and my eyes should be closed but they're not. Instead I feel the warm cement under my splayed arms and legs, and I'm looking up at the sky, my eyes first on the metal birds, then traveling upwards. I see a real bird flying overhead and maybe it sees me, too. Its wings are outstretched just like my body on the ground, and it's like we're both flying.

Around me the play finishes as Eunice carries a sign across that says "The End." Everyone claps. One by one, each player steps forward and the clapping swells—Amanda, Eunice, and Ezra (the guy in the glasses). When I get up, not only do people clap but they actually cheer "Whoa!" No one has done that for me before. I look around and everyone is smiling and clapping and yelling "Bravo!"

Shanthi comes up to me and pats me on the back.

"Good job, Lenny!" Amanda and Eunice say.

"Good job, Lenny," Ezra says, too.

They're all calling me Lenny, but I don't mind one bit.

Chapter 22

I'm officially obsessed with being Lenny. The lines from the play are in my head all the time.

"Can you pass the honey?" Mom asks at breakfast. "Make sure it doesn't drip."

"Yes, Ma. You tell me a *million* times."

"What? No, I don't. You just dripped it now."

"I *just* need a chance."

Mom stares at me blankly.

Then in the car.

"Ugh, this seat belt is too tight," Nitya complains. "Someone needs to fix it."

"That will be me!"

Nitya is less than impressed. "Are you high?" she asks me.

On the way home from the store, Dad is scratching his lottery ticket, and I say, "Carpe diem. Can't I do that?" just like Lenny does at the beginning of the play when he sees his piano for the first time. Wistful. Hoping. I use the same tone.

Before Dad can respond, there's a gust of wind and a flyer hits him in the face. I fall silent.

So far, Dad and I have been ignoring them. The flyers are

everywhere—yellow half-sheets stuck on telephone poles, on the sides of buildings, and even on the seats at the T stop. But now the half-sheet is literally in Dad's face, so he's forced to peel it off and look at it.

HOUSE OF CHAAT SO VERY THRILLED WITH YOUR PATRONAGE!

NOW ENJOY ALL-YOU-CAN-EAT SPECIAL JUST $5.99.

CAN'T STOP BY? NO PROBLEM! BUY OUR READY-TO-COOK ITEMS.

FRESH, DELICIOUS & READY IN 5 MINUTES!

HOUSE OF CHAAT MEANS: NO GROCERIES TO BUY,

MORE TIME FOR YOU!

"No groceries to buy!" Dad repeats angrily. He drops the flyer back on the ground. Mom would be furious. She's big on recycling.

"Maybe we should put up flyers, too," I say. It's been empty in the store. I'm sure he's noticed, and it seems like we have to do *something*. I feel a twinge of worry mixed with something else . . . guilt. I've been so distracted by the play and rehearsing that I haven't been thinking about the store. I'm even forgetting a few things when I pack the deliveries. Yesterday I forgot Mrs. Rodrigues's mangos. When I got to her place, she looked inside the empty bag and started laughing. But it's not just that. I'm forgetting my lists, too. Like the forty-fifth flavor of ice cream at Carmine's? I can't remember! The lines from the play are taking up all the room in my brain.

My dad is still glaring. "We don't need a flyer. We've been here for ten years. Everyone knows who we are."

I try to think of something to make him feel better. "Everyone needs groceries, Dad."

"That's right. How can you make anything in five minutes? It's a lie. It must be a sales ploy."

A minute later, we pass by House of Chaat, which seems, sales ploy or not, full of customers. In fact, some of them are our own customers, people who used to shop at our store. We pretend not to notice them. We pretend we have more important things to talk about, like hard work, or winning the lottery, or who's going to win the next World Cup in cricket.

Meanwhile, Dad's prediction seems to be coming true—the restaurant is drawing away our customers. The ones who want to eat things packed in Styrofoam, who don't want to cook unless it's done in five minutes, who might possibly not believe in hard work or the universe, or any of the other things my dad has held dear for so long. And Juhi's family? They're the Sharks or the Jets, or I don't know what. But one thing's for sure, they're the enemy.

"I *knew* about this," I whisper under my breath so my dad doesn't hear. The line is the only thing that makes me feel like the world is waiting for me.

Chapter 23

There are two more five-minute plays left, one on Thursday and one on Friday. I don't even plan to be there on Thursday. It just sort of happens because I have a delivery on campus around noon, so I'm at the plaza. Amanda and Eunice see me right away.

"It's Lenny!" Amanda says.

I'm glad they call out to me first. I wasn't going to say anything. I didn't want them to think I was a hanger-on. I wonder if Shanthi is here, but I don't see her. "What play are you doing?" I ask.

"*Camelot*," Amanda says. "It's another musical."

I don't want to ask but I can't help myself. "Is there something I could do?"

"Hey, yeah, we should get Lenny to do something," Eunice says.

Amanda says, "We can't pick him from the audience again. That wouldn't be fair, right?"

"That's okay." I try not to sound disappointed.

"He could do Ezra's part," Eunice suggests. "Ezra's only got one line, but he's sick today."

"Oh yeah, you can be Mordred," Amanda says. "You get to kill King Arthur."

"Cool," I say, brightening. "I have practice killing people."

She and Eunice laugh.

Amanda reads the line to me. "*Come, Dad, it's time for mortal combat.* Then you impale each other with a sword. It's not there in the original musical, but Eunice says she saw the ending of *Excalibur,* and Mordred and Arthur off each other there."

"Yeah, we thought we'd spice things up for Noon Day," Eunice says, grinning.

"Cool." I never realized that theater could be so violent.

Meanwhile, I am totally excited. At first I try not to show it. I don't want people thinking, *Lenny's excited to play dead!* Then I think, who cares, and I fly about getting ready.

The play starts with Amanda as King Arthur, who finds out that Sir Lancelot, his most famous knight of the Round Table, has secretly fallen in love with Queen Guinevere. I help out with the set (which is moving a cardboard box "castle" from one place to another). The group chooses a female Japanese tourist to play Guinevere. Her English is very careful, but she seems to be having a good time.

"How do the regular people hang out?" she asks haltingly. "They dance and watch TV and wonder how the royal people hang out."

"That's why I love you," says Lancelot (Eunice in a wig).

By the end of the play, it's discovered that Lancelot and Guinevere are having an affair. So Guinevere is going to be burned at the stake when Lancelot rescues her and they disappear, her to a nunnery, and I'm not sure where he goes. In the last scene, King Arthur's illegitimate son, Mordred (me), shows up, and he hates his father. Then he and Arthur have a duel and they kill each other with plastic knives.

So like yesterday, I find myself on the ground, this time as dead Mordred. Today it's overcast and I don't see birds while I'm lying there, just a milky white sky and the outlines of buildings. I can hear Eunice reciting the end, with the murmur of voices from the audience behind her, and car horns and the T rumbling past on the tracks, and amid all of that, my own heart. It's beating fast inside my rib cage. I think of my mom, who wanted to operate on this human organ. What would she think, seeing her son lying here, playing dead? That the heart pumps two thousand gallons of blood a day. That her kids need to be on the right path. That Lenny had the genes to be a musician, but me? What do I have the genes for? I blink. I try not to think of my mom.

Then Amanda pulls me up and we all take a bow, including the Japanese tourist. We smile and clap for each other. It's nice.

This time, I linger a little longer.

"You stoked about Shanthi's play?" Amanda asks me as I help them pack up.

"Yeah, it's cool," I say. "I've never acted before."

"You're great," Eunice says. "And you look just like Lenny Bernstein."

"Really?"

"Who the hell knows," Amanda says. "I've never seen him. Tomorrow we do *Little Shop of Horrors*. A plant that eats people."

"You want to come back and be a carnivorous plant?" Eunice asks.

"More killing people?" I ask.

"Hah," Amanda says. "You're good at it."

5-MINUTE PLAYS IN 5 PARTS

- No props except what you make with your hands.
- No lines except what you read off a piece of paper.
- No rehearsing . . . you just go.
- Who cares if you make a mistake?
- Tomorrow you do another.

♪

The next morning, I wait for Shanthi to call in her order. I want to tell her about the five-minute play yesterday. How it was the most fun I've ever had, how I'm not scared of being in front of people, how the exact words don't matter—they're just a bridge to being someone else. Yoshi Oida says words are like a diving board. That's how I feel. Like the words are taking me somewhere. But I haven't heard from Shanthi yet, which is strange because usually she'll have called by now. Maybe something came up.

So I deliver methi powder to House of Chaat, where I now see a "ready-to-cook" refrigerator in the front of the store. It's full of things like dosai batter, rolled-out rotis, chopped vegetables, and preassembled curries that require just five minutes of frying or heating. And people are clamoring to buy the stuff. Juhi says they barely have time to stock the refrigerator before it gets cleaned out. When she says that, I get a hole in my stomach thinking about our own pathetic refrigerator that's in danger of breaking down at any minute. Then I try not to think about it at all.

I go back to the store and still no word from Shanthi, so I take mangos to Mrs. R, who calls me inside for lassi, and I deliver twenty pounds of brown basmati rice to Mrs. Carmichael, who wants to talk about blood sugar levels, although what do I know about that? Then I deliver four ten-pound bags of atta flour, a bag of fresh okra, and some frozen goods to our other regulars, and I stop to see if Binh is around, but he's busy. Each time I come back to the store, still nothing, nothing, nothing from Shanthi.

"Karthik, what's going on?" Dad asks. I'm at the counter, and I guess he's been calling my name but I didn't hear him. "Your head is in the clouds."

On a piece of paper, I was doodling a picture of a plant with teeth. Last night I watched a video clip of the song "Feed Me" from *Little Shop of Horrors*. I've been wondering, how exactly do I play a man-eating plant? Yoshi Oida didn't have any acting advice for *that*.

"Did Shanthi call in her order?" I ask. It's already 11:30 and I still haven't heard from her. "Because usually she calls in for a bag of—"

"Spicy chips and two cans of Fanta," Dad finishes. "Yes, I know. And it's a waste of your time. I don't know what happens, but you're gone for hours afterward. So I told her we have a ten-dollar minimum on deliveries and that was that."

"Wait, what?" I stare at him in disbelief.

"Every time I look around, you're gone."

"That's not true," I say immediately, even though I know it is. I just didn't think he noticed. "And Shanthi needs those spicy chips. Did you know she's got a thesis to write? Those chips help her, um . . . concentrate."

"Then let her buy the family size!" Dad exclaims. "I want you back after every delivery, okay? That means House of Chaat or Mrs. Rodrigues or whoever else."

I feel sweat gather along my brow. I'm suddenly furious. If we really do this minimum thing, then I'm finished. How will Shanthi be able to order so much every day? As it is, I feel guilty she orders five dollars' worth of junk food every time we meet.

"What about Mrs. Rodrigues?" I point out. "She doesn't always order ten dollars. Neither does Mr. Jain. Neither do the other customers, and—"

"End of discussion. You have bags to deliver. Get to it."

For the first time, I hate the store. I hate that I'm stuck here and I have no choice, and maybe I even hate my dad. But I hold my tongue. I want to make the play at noon. This whole morning I've been racing back to the store to get everything delivered as soon as I get a list. I figure if I do that, Dad won't notice when I'm gone at lunch, as long as no one calls or shows up before I leave.

Around 11:42, I start to feel hopeful. So far, nobody. Then at 11:45, moments before I go on break, a tiny, elderly lady in a sari enters the store. She walks gingerly, her small feet moving feebly across the tiles until she reaches the counter. She puts her palms together. "Vanakkam," she says, the Tamil word for hello. "I hear you deliver?"

My heart sinks.

She tells us she lives around the corner. They are planning a "big, big puja" for blessings from Lord Rama. Can we help with a few items for her prayers?

"Of course!" Dad is beaming. "You have come to the right place."

"It is big, big puja," she repeats.

"We have all the time in the world," Dad says.

You might guess how this ends. How this miniature woman torches my lunch hour.

By the time we get everything she needs and I deliver them to her apartment for the "big, big" puja, the minutes have slipped away and it's twelve thirty. The last noonday five-minute play is over.

I'm so angry I can barely see. Suddenly I collide into someone on my way back from the little lady's apartment.

"Karthik!" Shanthi exclaims. She sees my face. "Hey, are you okay?"

"He . . . he just made me," I sputter. "And now Amanda and Eunice hate me, and . . ."

"Whoa. Hang on." Shanthi makes me sit on the steps of an apartment building and tell her everything slowly. I'm not even sure if she understands, but in the end she tells me not to worry.

"I was at BU," she says. "No one was mad. These things happen. But I'm surprised you went back and did another one." She sees my face. "I mean, in a good way! They all said you were great."

"Yeah?" I ask.

"Yeah. Some of the tourists even asked about you, like if you're in the program." Shanthi smiles. "Introducing the world's youngest Lenny Bernstein."

"Actually I was Mordred."

"You can be anything, Karthik."

"You mean as an actor?"

"I mean as *you*."

In front of us there is a traffic jam on Comm Ave and honking. We watch as people are yelling at one another from their cars.

"I'm sorry about the ten-dollar minimum," I say.

"Oh, that." She shrugs. "Consider it a donation to the Karthik Raghavan Actor Fund."

"No, I'll come even without any deliveries. I still get breaks."

I don't tell her the truth, which is that I *don't* have breaks. Not the way my dad is now watching me like a hawk. But I'll find a way around him. Because the play is important to Shanthi. And because I realize something else for the first time. The play is important to *me*.

WHY ACTING IS A BAD IDEA

- You have to look good under bright lights and tons of stage makeup.
- You have to live in New York or LA or one of those big cities full of other actors.
- You have to be around other actors and hear about their interesting lives.
- You might have to get an interesting life.
- If you play other characters, you might start changing, too.
- You might grow more confident, because that looks good on an actor.
- You might learn to project your voice (because that looks good on an actor, too).
- You might think the world is an interesting place with people like Shanthi in it.
- You won't want to be a doctor anymore (you never did).
- But now it's because there's something else you'd rather be.

Chapter 24

To celebrate India Independence Day, Dad is handing out free sweets at our counter. Everyone who shops at our store gets one square of mitthai. "Long live India," he tells the three customers we see in the store. There are mini Indian flags hung throughout the aisles: green, orange, and white stripes, with a blue wheel at the center. The symbol of hard work. Aasif is in charge of putting them up. By the afternoon, there are flies circling the sweets. I count them. There are more flies than customers. But we leave the sweets out anyway.

House of Chaat is celebrating Independence Day, too. Their ready-to-cook refrigerator is filled with packets of Independence Day pilaf (just bake and eat!) and paneer surprise (just fry and eat!), and at the counter you can order the special, which is an orange Fanta and green pakoras for two bucks. When I enter their kitchen with the dry ginger they ordered, everyone is in a frenzy. Outside, the line is the longest I've ever seen it.

"But I can fry the pakoras," Juhi is saying. "Let me help."

Satish Shah isn't having it. "We need you to pack. Look how many orders we have."

Juhi glares after he's gone. "See how he's bossing me around every second?" she says.

Behind her are different prepping stations. Some people are putting together the packets for the refrigerator outside. For the pakoras, there is a whole assembly line: one person mixes the batter, another fries the pakoras in oil, and another takes out the cooked pakoras and dries them in metal baskets. It feels like a highly organized circus.

"What makes the pakoras green?" I ask.

"Ground cilantro and mint. It's my recipe," Juhi says proudly.

Someone comes in from the back. "Are they ready? The bicycles are in."

"Shoot! We're so behind." Juhi looks at me for a moment. "Karthik, can you help?"

For the next several minutes, we pack boxes of pakora. It turns out there's a banquet at BU and they need one hundred boxes to go. Juhi and I don't even talk, we just pack. The order has to be delivered by three o'clock. The whole time it's not lost on me that I'm packing boxes for my dad's competition. It's not lost on me that we have our own deliveries to do instead. I sigh. I'm a dweeb.

Outside in the alley, Juhi and I load up the boxes on the backs of the shiny new bicycles. One box on top of another and another, and then strapped with stretchy rope and covered with a nylon sheet. The two bicyclists are teenage boys from Bangladesh not much older than me, and they have bells attached to their bikes. *Ring ring!* The metal bells sound funny, and Juhi and I crack up when we try them out. When the bicyclists set out on the sidewalk, we can hear the bells ringing all the way to the end of Harvard Ave. *Ring ring! Make way for pakoras!*

The brick feels hot on my back as Juhi and I stand shoulder-to-shoulder against the alley wall. She saved a box of pakoras for us, and we eat them together quickly before Satish Shah finds us outside. In my mouth there is an explosion of steam from the hot pakoras and the flavor of onions, chilies, mint, and spices. I have my music player with me, so I turn it up to full volume while we eat, and we can hear the soundtrack to *West Side Story* blasting from my headphones down the alley.

Juhi and I sing along in thick Indian accents, and after a while we're laughing so hard we can't sing anymore.

"Isn't this the best?" she asks, leaning against me.

Hot weather. Hot brick. Hot pakoras.

And I don't want the summer to end.

♪

In the evening, I'm on my bed playing solitaire when my mom comes in with a news article. It's the same one she put in my backpack two days ago. I'd left it on the couch.

"I'm busy," I say. I have three cards left and they all have to be reds for me to win.

"You're playing a card game."

"I'm almost done."

She watches me. "You'll never win. The odds are against you."

Coming from anyone else, that would be sour grapes. But who do you think taught me to play in the first place? "Sometimes odds don't matter," I say.

She studies me. "There's something different about you, Cutie." She reaches to move my hair, but I twist back so she misses. "Is it your hair? Or I don't know what."

"Nothing's different," I say, but my heart starts beating fast. It's like my mom is going to figure it out, that I'm in a play and didn't tell her, that I love something she doesn't know. She's sharp. She can sniff out guilt. Is that what it is? I'm feeling guilty?

She holds up the article. "Let's talk about this."

I fall back on my pillow and groan. "Can we do that, like, never?"

"I bet you didn't even read it," she says.

"I did. I don't want to talk about the Financial Crisis." I stare at my faded Major League Baseball bedspread. It was on sale at Target, and one day in fourth grade, I counted up all the team logos (thirty). "Your dad went broke but you turned out fine," I tell her. "Leonard Bernstein lived through the Great Depression. And he became famous."

"That's what you think? You're going to be the next Leonard Bernstein? Did you read the ending of that book? Because I did. And guess what? He died very lonely. His wife gone. His kids gone—"

I sit up. "But that has nothing to do with the Great Depression! Or the Financial Crisis."

Mom looks at me, and for a second I think it's because I've changed her mind. Then she says, "You kids think you can do anything. You think the world is going to give you what you want."

I watch her leave my room and I wonder, *What's wrong with that?*

WHY I LIKE ACTING IN SHANTHI'S PLAY

- Not worrying about the Financial Crisis
- Not thinking about bone glue or heart surgery
- Throwing my head back when I laugh
- I *knew* about this!
- Fake-playing the piano
- Hair gel
- Being Lenny (not me)

Chapter 25

"The last scene is the most important one in the play," Shanthi says at our next rehearsal. "It's what you leave your audience with. What they savor last."

"Like dessert." Just saying that makes my stomach grumble. It's been hard to get to her apartment with Dad's new ten-dollar-minimum rule, not to mention him watching my every move. Today I skipped lunch so I could rehearse. I don't want Shanthi feeling bad, so I haven't told her. But that doesn't stop me from thinking about food.

"More than that," she tells me. "Dessert is sweet. Theater is reflective. It stays in our minds. Like dreams."

"Right," I say. So much for my food analogy.

We've gone over the last scene ten times today and Shanthi has hated every take of it. I think she's worried about the play. So am I. Summer's almost over, and we haven't been able to rehearse much. Juhi says she wants to come to the performance, but do I want her there? Do I want anyone? I'm desperately hoping my family never finds out about it.

"Are you inviting your parents to the performance?" I ask.

"Why would I do that?" Shanthi's cat eyes flash, which means end of the discussion. "Also, we need to run this in front of somebody."

"You mean your advisor?"

"No. Call your best friend. Miles. And didn't you mention a girl? Call her, too. The one who said to gel your hair."

"Wait, what?" I look at her in alarm.

"I thought you liked doing the five-minute plays," Shanthi says, surprised.

"Yeah, but that was different. I didn't know anybody!"

"You have to practice in front of people you know," she says. "You also need to rehearse with the actors playing Sam and Jeannie. We'll do that in September when school is back in session. But for now, you need to get used to people watching you. If you were in an acting class, you would be doing stuff in front of students all the time. The audience is part of a play—they give you energy. And your friends being there will give you *tons* more energy."

I think of the crowd at BU when I was fake-killing people. Were they giving me energy? They were smiling and laughing, but they might have been thinking, who is this chump?

Shanthi smiles gently. "I bet Lenny got cold feet when he had to perform, too."

"He wore those cuff links," I say.

"What?"

In the Bernstein book, I read that Lenny had a pair of gold cuff links he got from Serge Koussevitzky, the conductor for the Boston Symphony.

"The ones from Koussevitzky. Lenny kissed them for good luck before he went onstage."

Shanthi blinks. "Okaaay. I guess I don't remember everything I read, like some people."

"It was in a sidebar," I say, which makes her roll her eyes.

When I read about the cuff links, I had to look them up online, because I didn't know what they were. I was even wondering if I could get a pair. Then I saw they're like little buttons to keep your fancy shirtsleeves all nice and pinned together. So forget that—I barely own a dress shirt.

"So when do you want my friends over?" I ask. I think of Miles and Juhi watching me and my stomach churns all over again. Back to reality.

"Let's do Friday," Shanthi says. "It will be like a pre-dress rehearsal. I can't wait! Remember, it's all about drawing energy."

PRE-DRESS REHEARSAL IN 3 PARTS

- Lights
- Action
- Barfing

Is that the energy Shanthi's talking about?

Chapter 26

I get why Shanthi wants me to practice in front of my friends. She wants to know if I'll choke onstage. I guess I want to know that, too. Yoshi Oida says the audience helps you figure out what you're doing in the first place. Which is good, because I need all the help I can get.

When I tell Juhi about the pre-dress rehearsal, she's very excited.

"Of course, I'll come!" she says, and jumps up and down in the kitchen so that the other cooks stare at her. She says she'll get time off. I'm not sure why she cares so much. The idea of her there still makes me feel like barfing.

At the store, Miles is more subdued. "Cool. Binh, too, right?"

Shanthi had only mentioned the two of them. But I guess it's okay if Binh comes.

"Sure," I say. Maybe if he's there, no one will laugh. Binh is nice that way.

Meanwhile, Dad comes to the counter with a small bag. "For Mr. Jain," he says.

"Mr. Jain?" We haven't heard from him in a long time.

"Yes," Dad says. "You better run it to him right now."

The bag looks small and I want to ask, what about the ten-dollar minimum? But something tells me not to. I look inside the bag. There's a packet of Insta Noodles and two apples. No tea. It's not the usual order. In the back room, we can hear the phone ringing. No one is answering it.

"Where's Aasif?" I ask. Usually he picks up on the first ring.

"He's not here," Dad says. "Why don't you get that bag to Mr. Jain."

"I'll walk with you," Miles says. "I have to meet my mom downtown."

Outside, it's overcast and muggy. I don't bother getting the bike out. Mr. Jain is only a block away.

"My dad is looking for another job," Miles says.

It takes me a moment to register. "You mean . . . ?"

Miles shrugs. "They let everyone go in his group. I guess he knew it was coming."

"I'm sorry, Miles."

"Yeah, well."

Wow, Miles's dad lost his job. I think about my dad all over again and a feeling of dread comes over me. We don't say anything for a while as we keep walking.

"Also he's not sure he wants to be a plumber anymore," Miles finally says.

"Yeah?"

"Yeah." He pushes his glasses up. "He's looking at a few things. We might move."

"Really?"

"Don't tell anyone."

Who would I tell? I guess he means Binh. But why not tell him? We can see the T coming up slowly along the tracks.

"Gotta go," Miles says.

He crosses the street to the island where the T stop is. He's wearing his faded gray Red Sox shirt and orange Nikes. I was with him when he bought both. The Nikes were on sale at Moody's, and his mom said orange is a terrible color, but Miles wanted them anyway. Afterward, Miles and I had ice cream cones at Kenmore Square while his mom smoked a cigarette. She's the only person I know who smokes. And she's a dental hygienist.

The gray shirt Miles got at Fenway. Spencer had an extra ticket, so I went with Miles's family and watched the Red Sox cream the Baltimore Orioles, though I spent the last inning in the bathroom throwing up after eating too much cotton candy. It's strange how Miles's outfit can have so many memories attached to it. I watch him get on the T, pushing his glasses up one more time before the doors close behind him. *Short, glasses, crossword.* He's still all of that. But he's more.

I'll hate it if he moves.

♪

When I ring Mr. J's door, he buzzes me in right away without asking who it is. I guess he's expecting me. His door is already open when I go inside.

"Hey Mr. Jain, long time no . . ." I stop. Mr. Jain is on the couch and his foot is in a cast. He looks at me, vexed, his face gray and unshaven. "Mr. Jain! What happened?"

"Seventy-eight years," he declares, "not a scratch, not a trip to the hospital, not a thing wrong with me. Then yesterday on the front step of my apartment, what do I do? Someone should fix that crack. I have complained to the management. Maybe I should sue them as well."

"You fell down?" I ask.

"Hairline fracture," he says. "Two weeks cast, three weeks boot, one month physical therapy. Not to mention a lifetime of boredom and misery."

"Where should I put this?" I hold the bag up.

"Oh, that. Put it in the kitchen, if you don't mind. And when you're there, can you start some water on the stove? There should be a saucepan. Just fill it with water and start the stove. I'll come over when the water is boiling."

The kitchen is to the right of the door, and inside, it's a mess. There are dirty dishes piled up in the sink and the dining table is unclean with a half-eaten plate of food still on it. The drapes are drawn and there is day-old bread left on a cutting board with crumbs everywhere. My mom would be aghast. I have never seen our kitchen this way. Even when my mom had the flu two years ago, she swept the floor and put all the dishes away, and in the evening there was dal and hot rotis on the table.

I look for the saucepan Mr. Jain is talking about. There's one with water in it already on the back burner.

"Did you find it?" He calls from the living room.

"Yeah, it's right here."

"Good. Just start the water. Then you can go. I'll have Insta Noodles for lunch."

Under no circumstances will Mom let Nitya and me have Insta Noodles, because it's "pure junk" and "full of MSG." But Dad brings it home from the store anyway, and any time Mom is gone on an errand, Nitya and I will make it for ourselves. It might be pure junk and kill us before we're fifty, but it still tastes delicious.

I pour out the old water and put in some fresh water and heat it on the stove.

"Let me wait until the water is boiling. I'll throw everything in for you."

"Are you sure?" Mr. Jain asks. "That's very kind. It's hard to get around with this cast."

"Yeah, no problem."

As I'm waiting for the water to boil, I load the dishes in the dishwasher, even though at home I almost never do it until my mom is breathing down my neck. But here, there's no room to drain the noodles when they're done unless I clear the sink. And then because I'm doing that, I might as well clean off the counter and table, where there are several empty Styrofoam boxes I recognize from House of Chaat. Then, before I know it, I'm bringing Mr. Jain a bowl of cooked Insta Noodles, some sliced apples on the side, and a cup of hot tea.

He says his daughter is coming at the end of the day to check up on him. He says everything is under control. He says at his age a hairline fracture is nothing. He knows people who have to get hip replacement surgery or stents put in their arteries or they have to breathe with an oxygen tank.

"I'm so much luckier, so much better off," he tells me. When he eats his noodles, he sucks them up noisily. There is tea spilled around his cup. He tells me that the noodles are delicious, like the kind he used to eat when he was a boy. He doesn't mention the papdi chaat from House of Chaat that tastes like India, or the ready-to-cook items that were packed in the Styrofoam boxes. Instead, he's happy with the Insta Noodles. And me sitting on the couch.

He talks about how India is definitely going to the World Cup next time around, how autumn in New England is the best, not too hot, not too cold, and how his cast will be off by then, and his daughter will take him to New Hampshire to look at the fall colors. It's strange that I didn't know he had a daughter before. I tell him how my mom and sister like the fall colors, too. It's not exactly the truth. (Mom has to drag all of us out in the minivan to drive on the Kancamagus Highway every October and Nitya bitterly complains, though she always ends up taking a bunch of pictures.) But Mr. J listens to everything I say, and I guess it's nice.

By the time I leave, it's an hour later. And I don't know why I did all the things I did for Mr. Jain. But it's like with the Mrs. Rodrigueses and the mangos. It just happens, and then people seem to change. Mr. Jain already has. When I step out, he's reading the newspaper and there's color in his cheeks, and sunlight is coming in his room through the window.

Saturday evening, my cousin Raj is back. This time it's because of a wedding in Philadelphia that my aunt and uncle are attending. After my parents go to bed, Nitya, Raj, and I stretch out on the couch while Raj flips to late-night TV.

"So, Karthu, man of the hour," he says, "what's the deal with Juhi?"

I stiffen. Is he ever going to let that go? That was, like, last month.

"Nothing," I say.

"Juhi?" Nitya asks Raj. "You mean Asha Shah's sister?"

"The one and only," Raj says. "Karthik was spending quality time with her last time I saw."

"At my dance recital?" Nitya turns to me. "You got something going with Juhi?"

Raj snickers. "He wishes. Karthik, man of the hour."

I glare at him. "Stop saying that."

Nitya is watching with interest. "So what if he likes her? I think it's cute. What? Why are you both looking at me like that?"

My sister seems to be in some weird, nice zone. I'd rather she called me a dweeb.

"She's just a friend," I say.

"Not the 'friend friend.'" Raj hooks his thick fingers to make quotes in the air.

"Why, don't you have any?" I ask coolly.

"Take it from me. You don't want to be her friend. If she's anything like Asha Shah—let me guess, she's got a white boyfriend."

"Of course not," I say. But Raj sees my face.

"I'm right, I know it. So she's got this boyfriend. Which means she's only nice to you when he isn't there."

"That isn't true. She—"

"And she's only nice when it's just you two, but forget it if her other friends are around."

Nitya tells me, "Don't listen to Raj. He's mad because he asked Asha out and she said no. She's going out with a basketball player."

"Hey," he says. "It's lacrosse."

Nitya rolls her eyes. "Sorry. Lacrosse."

I listen to Nitya and Raj go back and forth. It seems like they've had this conversation before. "Can I have the remote?" I ask.

Raj ignores my request. "Stay away from Juhi Shah. You won't get any action."

"Gross." Nitya takes the remote from him. "Like I said, don't listen to Raj."

"It doesn't matter," Raj says. "Indian chicks don't want to date Indian guys."

As soon as he says that, my antenna goes up. There it is again: Indian guys, and what's wrong with them. Only what I don't get is, why are Raj and I on the same side of the equation? I mean, look at him. Raj is sprawled across the couch, scratching his bottom without shame.

Meanwhile, Nitya is flipping channels and stops on *Scary Movie 3*.

"Ooh, this is the good one," Raj says. "Where they do *Dead Again*."

"I'm sorry, did you say 'Indian chicks'?" Nitya asks.

"It's not *Dead Again*," I say. "It's *The Sixth Sense*. They spoof *The Sixth Sense*."

"I see dead people. Same difference." Raj turns to Nitya. "'Indian chick' is a universal term."

"There's a reason Indian girls don't date Indian guys," Nitya says.

"Because they use the term 'Indian chick'?" He lets out a burp and grins. "Excuse me."

"Because they're *clueless*!"

I'm trying to concentrate on *Scary Movie 3*. It's the funeral scene, which is usually funny, but I'm finding it hard to laugh, listening to Nitya and Raj. Because it sounds like Nitya is supporting me, when actually she's saying the same thing as Juhi: *Indian guys aren't*.

"You're being racist," I say.

"No, I'm not, Dweeb." Nitya looks at me, surprised.

Well, at least we're back to Dweeb. But she's not off the hook.

"Saying you won't date someone because they're Indian is racist," I say.

"Tell it to her, man," Raj says, grinning.

Nitya sputters, not coming up with a good response. You can tell she hates being called a racist, especially from the two of us.

"Maybe you should take a good look at yourself in the mirror," I say.

"Maybe you should take a hike," Nitya shoots back.

Raj's eyes are on the TV, and he calls out, "She's going to punch him. Watch! This is the good part." We all wait for the punch, in spite of ourselves. Then the TV goes blank.

"Great," Nitya says.

"Your TV bites," Raj says. "This happens every time."

"This *never* happens," Nitya says. "No wonder. You're sitting on the remote, Raj."

He turns the TV back on, but now the punch scene is over and Raj and Nitya have moved on from Indian guys and are talking about studying for the SAT.

Meanwhile, I'm no closer to understanding what's so wrong with me.

Chapter 27

The next morning, I'm eating a bowl of Cheerios when my dad walks into the kitchen still wearing his light blue pajamas. "There's been a change in plans," he says. "I'm not going to the store today."

I'm surprised. Usually Dad is dressed and ready to go by the crack of dawn. I was wondering where he was. "You've got a doctor's appointment?" I ask. Which would also be weird. He never goes to the doctor. In fact, I can't remember the last time he was sick.

"No, no, just some stuff to take care of at home."

By now, Mom comes in and says, "Paperwork, Cutie." She starts making coffee.

"Paperwork?" Now this sounds suspicious, especially with Mom doing the explaining. "Are you sure it isn't a doctor's appointment?" Maybe there's something wrong, like with Dad's heart, and they're covering it up. For a moment I reflect on what my mom always says, how it would be good to have a doctor in the family. She's right. For times like this. Someone could whip out a stethoscope or fill out a speedy prescription for antibiotics. Leave it to Nitya to pick something useless like law.

But Mom brushes me off. "Don't be ridiculous," she says.

The way she says that I'm relieved. Still, it's strange for my dad to stay home. "Did you tell Aasif? Is he back from his trip?"

"Aasif isn't at the store," Dad says shortly.

"That's what you said before. What do you mean?"

Dad avoids my eyes. Then it hits me.

"Wait, you fired Aasif? You *fired* Aasif?"

He looks pained. "You don't understand, Karthik. I had no other choice."

"But all the deliveries . . ." I stop. I realize now they weren't helping. They probably never did. Maybe that's why Dad isn't going to the store today. Because he can't stand the awful reality of everything.

I look down at my bowl of Cheerios, at the circles floating in milk like little buoys. When I was six, Aasif used to save bubble gum wrappers for when Nitya and I came to the store, then twist the wrappers into dolls for us. We still have them on a shelf at home. Now Aasif is gone.

Dad watches me. "Karthu, maybe when we're doing better in the fall, I can hire him back."

Do better in the fall? What's he talking about? Every day there are fewer customers, the refrigerator is broken, and now we've lost our accountant. I eat my Cheerios silently. The entire morning has been upended and I haven't even finished breakfast. Then I'm hit by another grim thought. "If Aasif is gone, and you're not going in, then who's running the store?"

"Take a guess," Mom says.

I feel the Cheerios sink to the bottom of my stomach.

3 WAYS MOM IS DIFFERENT FROM DAD

- On the T, she uses hand sanitizer and Kleenex to wipe down the seats.
- She knits the whole time, even when she's standing.
- She says hi to the other Indians she sees (half of them are too surprised to say hi back).

At the store, I discover that Mom likes to be in charge of everything. And by everything, I mean *everything*.

"Wash your hands, Cutie. Keep the papers off the counter. Keep the bags ready. And stop chewing gum. You know that's bad for you. Miles, hello, what are you doing here?"

Miles looks bewildered to see my mother at the counter.

"Uh, nothing, Mrs. Raghavan. Just hanging out with Karthik."

When my mom steps away, Miles tells me they were out of cereal at home, so he was hoping to score a frozen samosa at the store for breakfast. I heat up one for him as he sits down next to me.

"How's your dad?" I ask him.

"Eh," Miles says. He looks different. He's more tan and his nose and ears are red. He sees me looking at him. "We were at the Cape all weekend," he explains. "My uncle owns a boat."

"Is this your Uncle Milton who got fired?"

"Yeah, well, he still has a boat. What's he supposed to do with it?"

He could sell it. But I don't say that. The microwave beeps and I hand him the samosa on a paper plate.

"What's your mom doing here?" he finally asks as he's chewing.

"Long story," I say, because I still don't actually know why she's here and my dad is doing "stuff" at home.

When Mom comes back to the counter with a clipboard, she says, "Cutie, did you see the delivery list? Someone named Mrs. Rodrigues wants—"

"Yeah, I know it already." I get the mangos from the bin. Mom watches while I hold different ones, feeling and smelling them until I find the two best.

"Where did you learn that?" she asks. "That's how my mother picked fruit at the market."

"I'm not clueless."

"Should I leave?" Miles whispers to me as I walk by. I glance at my mom. I have no idea what she'll do or say to him while I'm gone. She might make him sweep the floor or stack paper bags, or worse. "Nah," I tell him. "You'll be fine."

♪

"This mango lassi is getting better and better each time," Mrs. Rodrigues says. "You are doing a great job, Karthik."

"He is a mango farmer!" Mrs. Rodrigues's mother-in-law exclaims. Rani the parrot squawks in agreement.

A strange transformation has taken place in their household in the last few visits. The same Mrs. R who was *cheap, mango, broken buzzer* now can't wait to bring me a cup of lassi along with tea biscuits or other cookies. She and her mother-in-law smile at me all the time, and not only that, they suddenly want to know everything about me, how old I am, what grade I'm in, what I want to study. They're fascinated I can remember lists. They have me close my eyes and tell them everything I can remember in the room, right down to what's in Rani's cage (a mirror, a swing, a miniature fake coconut tree). They've taught me the words to their favorite Hindi songs and are amazed I can sing the lyrics back to them. In a way I'm like their parrot, only I can do more tricks than Rani. Mostly, they're just glad to see me.

Today though, my mind begins to wander while they chat with me. I'm thinking of Aasif, who no longer has a job. What will happen to him? Does he even have a family? I never thought to ask him, and now I don't know if I'll ever see him again.

"What's wrong, Karthik? You are not looking like yourself," the mother-in-law says.

"Yes, something is bothering you," Mrs. Rodrigues says.

I set down my teacup and uneaten biscuit. "Nothing. I'm fine. Just full, I guess."

Then I sing their favorite song, "Kabhi Kabhie Mere Dil Mein." I've sung it before, but this time when I'm done, I ask them what the song means.

"It's from an old Hindi movie," Mrs. Rodrigues says. "I still remember when it came out in the theaters. That song was a hit, everyone was singing it."

"'Kabhi Kabhie Mere Dil Mein,'" the older Mrs. Rodrigues says, "is a song about the heart. About the feelings that come. This man, he is singing to his love. He is surprised she is there, that she was living in the stars and now has come to the earth to be his. And how does he know? His heart tells him."

Why is it always about the heart?

"Do they stay together?" I ask.

"Of course not," Mrs. Rodrigues says. "The best stories are never happy."

"That's not true," says the older Mrs. R.

"You know it is," the younger Mrs. R says. "I don't even have to debate it."

As they're talking, I'm reminded of *West Side Story* and Tony getting killed and Maria asking who will be next? I also think of what my mom said the other night, about Lenny dying lonely and sad. She's right. I'd skimmed that section of the book, about him in his seventies, barely being able to conduct his last concert at Tanglewood, and then dying a few months later in his New York apartment. I'd hated reading that part. I'm glad Shanthi's play ends with Lenny when he's young, at his recital, wowing everyone. I like imagining that Lenny instead, the one ready to take on the world.

Chapter 28

I'd gotten so caught up at Mrs. Rodrigues's I forgot about Mom and Miles. I hurry back to the store, expecting Miles to be on his knees, scrubbing the floor with his bare hands. Instead he's at the counter with my mom, doing the crossword. Not only that, they're sharing a packet of peanuts.

"What took you so long?" Mom asks. "How long does it take to deliver two mangos?"

"It's because he talks to those people," Miles explains. I had told him about the two Mrs. Rodrigueses and their parrot. "And they make him things to eat."

"What?" Mom says.

"And the other guy who broke his foot, Karthik cooks for him." Mom blinks.

"I made Insta Noodles for Mr. Jain," I say quickly. "And that was just once." I don't mention the sandwiches I've been making for him, too. They're pretty easy—Mr. J likes peanut butter and jelly with the crusts cut off. The only hard part is listening to him talk about cricket, but I run through my lines in my head while he does.

"Cutie, who are all these people?"

"Nobody, Mom. Just a few customers. They're lonely and I'm just being nice, okay?"

Mom's face softens. "It's sweet you talk to them. But you don't have to."

"I know that." I glance at Miles, worried he'll spill the beans about Shanthi. But Miles has returned his attention to the crossword.

"Four down doesn't work," he says. "We wrote salmon, but that's not right."

"Salmon is right," Mom says. "Four across is wrong. It's salivary, see?"

"Omigod, you're totally right."

"That's the only way two down works."

They keep going on, and I have no idea what they're talking about. I'm even slightly weirded out that they're getting along as well as they are. Then I notice Miles's thumb is bandaged with gauze. "What happened to you?"

Miles holds up his thumb. "I got a splinter when I dropped a glass jar."

"A splinter. You mean like *glass*?"

"It was large," Mom says. "Easy to see. I used tweezers from the first aid kit to get it out. I cleaned it first with hand sanitizer, then pulled that puppy out and dressed the wound. Done."

"Lots of blood dripping everywhere, even on the ground," Miles says, relishing the details.

Meanwhile, I feel like I might pass out. "Um, let's like *not* talk about it."

"He hates blood," Mom tells Miles. "This one time in the playground, his sister—"

"Can we not talk about that either?" I say.

"Mum's the word," Mom says. "By the way, that playwriting girl, Shanthi, called in an order."

"Oh?" I ask. So far, she hasn't ordered anything all week, thanks to Dad's new rule.

"Three bottles of Fanta and five bags of chips. How does anyone eat so much junk?"

"Bet it's ten dollars' worth," Miles says, and gives me a significant look.

"She's a student," I say, ignoring Miles. "Maybe that's all she can afford."

"She should have thought about that before she did playwriting," Mom observes.

When she's in the back room, Miles twirls his pencil. "She doesn't know about the play?"

"You saw how she is. She'd freak out."

"What's wrong with a play? It's not drugs."

"I know. She just likes to be in control of everything." I pack up Shanthi's groceries.

"At least she's good at the crossword," Miles tells me. "My mom wants to give me a fluoride rinse. And trust me, you'd rather do the crossword."

When I get to Shanthi's, she says she ordered because she wants to go over the plan for Friday with me. "Good news, Amanda and Ezra are coming to help out so you can practice rehearsing with other actors. That will get you ready for September when you have to do it for real with the actors the department lines up for my production. You remember Amanda and Ezra, right?"

"Yeah. From the five-minute plays." I look around Shanthi's small apartment, where there are stacks of books and a row of wilty plants on the floor next to the tiny dining table, and wonder how we will all fit in here.

"Are your friends coming, too?" she asks.

Just thinking about them makes my stomach flip. "Yeah. Can I bring Binh? He's another friend."

"Sure. The more the merrier."

I watch as she ticks off items from her checklist. Half of them are already crossed off and I see other things like "Call the theater," "Meet with advisor," and "Check with lighting."

Wow—this is really happening, the play is actually coming together. I see how serious Shanthi is with her checklist. Even if her plants aren't watered and she isn't talking to her parents, I can tell she's on top of things. She wants the play to be a success.

We decide to run through the last scene, which is at Lenny's recital. I sit down at Shanthi's piano.

"No, after the recital." She grins. "Even though you love fake-playing the Grieg piano concerto."

"The beginning is so epic. It sounds like thunder and lightning."

"Lightning isn't a sound," Shanthi says. "But I know what you mean. Let's start where you come up to Sam and Jennie at the end of the recital."

I nod and close my eyes. I always need a few moments to find Lenny. I go through my list: shoulders back, large hands, throws his head back when he laughs. I also think about his piano from Aunt Clara, how it was everything to him, and perfect, even if it was old and scratched up and some of the keys probably stuck. Then I open my eyes and I say my lines.

"Did you like it?" I ask. "Did you both like it?"

"You were terrific," Shanthi says, being Jennie.

"Yes, terrific," she says, switching to Sam.

"Then what's wrong, Dad? You look like you ate something bad."

"I don't want to be around, Lenny, when the world breaks your heart."

"Oh, stop," Shanthi says as Jennie. "The world will love Lenny. The world won't be big enough to hold him."

"Just wait," I say. "The world will be ready. I *know* about this."

I walk back to the piano.

Shanthi switches to Sam. "Lenny's brilliant," she says, "and for that, I'm afraid."

We wait a moment, her standing there, me at the piano. Shanthi says we should freeze so the audience knows it's the end.

"I have a question," I say when we're done freezing.

"Shoot."

It's the question I've always wondered about, but this time I remember to ask.

"Why does Sam say he's afraid?"

"He's afraid that music won't bring Lenny happiness." Shanthi scribbles something down on her checklist. "I just remembered, I have to tell Ezra to bring a stage mic."

"The book said Lenny died heartbroken because he thought no one would remember that he played the piano and wrote music, too. They would just remember he was a conductor."

"True," Shanthi said, still scribbling.

"So Sam *is* right," I say.

Shanthi looks up from her list now. "Well, I never said it was a happy play. Okay, let's go over the last scene again. Remember, be sure you're looking at Sam when you say your last line. He's the one worried about Lenny not being happy. Not the audience. Good old dad."

Meanwhile, I can't believe what Shanthi just said. Are there no happy endings at all?

WHY ACTING IS A BAD IDEA—PART 2

- If you succeed, you won't want to do anything else.
- If you fail, you won't want to do anything else either.

Chapter 29

The rest of the day I think about happy endings and sad endings. I think about acting and not acting. It all gets jumbled in my head. Even when I make lists, I still can't figure anything out.

At eleven at night, Nitya locks herself in the bathroom, crying and saying she isn't going to the SAT. For almost an hour, my mom scolds, begs, and pleads with her to come out. "Baby, it's just a test."

"It's not just a test. It's everything. It's you always telling me what to do. What if I don't want to be a lawyer?" Nitya's voice gets louder and louder. "What if I don't want to go to college?"

"Baby, it's about doing your best."

"Stop calling me Baby!" Nitya yells.

Eventually, Mom gives up and goes to bed. Dad is already asleep, although I don't know how he can sleep through all that racket. Finally it's quiet in the apartment except for the sound of Nitya's sniffling in the bathroom.

For a while I go over my lines for the play. Then I practice fake-playing the piano on the kitchen table, and it's a good thing nobody is around to see me because I look really goofy. Around midnight, I knock on the bathroom door.

"Come out, I have to pee," I say. I don't, but I figure it's one way to get my sister out. She's been in there long enough.

"Go away," Nitya mumbles.

"I'll have an accident," I say. "And then you'll really be in trouble."

"Very funny." The door remains closed. I can hear her blowing her nose.

"If you open up, I'll tell you why you won't be taking the SAT tomorrow."

Complete silence. A few seconds pass and Nitya opens the door.

"This better be good," she says.

"Your test is on Saturday." I put my hands in my pockets. "I just saw the admission ticket on the bulletin board in the kitchen. Does nobody look at that thing?"

"Mom told me it was tomorrow."

"She's wrong."

Nitya thinks for a moment, then slides to the floor in relief. "Thank god."

I sit down too, in the hallway next to the door. I'm tired, and so is Nitya. I guess we should go to bed. But neither of us feel like moving.

"Do you really not want to go to college?" I ask.

"Of course not. I just said that to scare her." Nitya creeps forward to lean against the door frame. "I wish Mom would leave me alone. I wish she would leave you alone, too."

We continue sitting on either side of the bathroom door, whispering to each other. It's been so long since I've talked to Nitya I've almost forgotten what it's like. Just a few years ago, we used to build forts under the dining table and watch *Star Wars* on TV. We got Mom to buy us ice cream from Star Market, the kind that was eggless because it's the only one Mom will buy. We would eat it with two spoons out of the same container and play Battleship and Uno and Mastermind. But that all stopped when Nitya started high school.

"If you weren't going to be a lawyer, what would you be?" I ask. "What's your dream?"

"Ugh. That's like those dippy essay questions I have to write for my college applications. Next."

I stare at the ground. She always does that. That's why I never tell her anything. That's why I haven't told her about the play. She'd probably shoot that down, too.

Nitya must sense I'm annoyed. "Sorry, Karthu. I guess I'm not sure. But this is what I've figured out. Whatever we do, whatever our dream is, we have to actively rebel against them."

"Who?"

"Mom and Dad. They mean well, but it's the job of every parent to crush the dreams of their children."

"How are they crushing our dreams? You don't even know what your dream is."

"It doesn't matter. They're going to crush it anyway. Mom doesn't believe we can think for ourselves, so she wants to do it for us."

"She's just afraid," I say. "Because of the Financial Crisis."

"Look, there will always be a financial crisis. Or a factory layoff. Or the flu. But that doesn't mean we shouldn't dream. We're kids. We're *supposed* to dream. Mom and Dad—they're the ones past dreaming."

I study Nitya. *Short, debates a lot, hair.* She's like a short, grouchy version of Lenny Bernstein. Lenny wanted to do his own thing, too, and he didn't care what his parents told him either.

"Don't you get it, Karthu?" she says. "We *have* to rebel. It's the only way to survive."

After she goes to bed, I take out the Bernstein book. I don't read. I keep flipping pages until I get to my favorite picture. It's one of Lenny when he's eighteen and playing the piano. One hand is on the keyboard and the other is straight up above his head. It's a grand flourish, his signature move. I've seen him do that in videos, where a single note launches his arm up into space, even before the phrase is over and he has to hit the next note correctly. How does he know he'll land right? It doesn't seem to matter to him. It's all about the power of music. And confidence.

I study the page for a long time, because *this* is what I want. I want to be that confident, without listening to Nitya or anyone else. I want to throw my arm up, not worrying whether my hand will land back on the next note.

That must be what dreams are about. About the beginning of things, not the end.

Chapter 30

The next morning, my dad says he needs to go to the bank, so he won't be coming to the store today either. I see him in the bathroom, shaving solemnly, which seems unnecessary before going to a bank. There's also a fresh shirt and tie laid out on the bed. Did my mom do that? Who knows. They're both acting weird, frankly.

So I go with my mom to the store for the second day in a row. When we get there, we find a message from Mrs. Rodrigues on our store phone. For the first time, she doesn't order mangos. She says she doesn't need any this morning.

"What, Cutie, you look disappointed," Mom says. "You like going over there."

"No, I don't," I say quickly. "They have this bird that squawks at me."

We look up to see Miles come in. Mom sets down her clipboard. "Mr. Miles, I have something for you," she says.

Miles puts down his backpack. "You mean the article, Mrs. Raghavan?"

"No, something better." She reaches into her bag and pulls out a book. "It's called *History of Horse Racing in America*. I forgot I had this. It's now yours."

I'm dumbstruck. Since when does my mom own books on racing? But judging from the beat-up way it looks, she's had the book for a long time. I guess I never saw it before.

"Wow, thanks," Miles says. He flips through the pages. "Is there stuff on Seabiscuit?"

"Seabiscuit?" I ask.

"A horse. My grandfather told me stories about seeing Seabiscuit race when he was little."

"Lots of stuff about Seabiscuit," Mom says to Miles.

And then they get into a conversation about racehorses, and I have no idea what they're talking about. I've barely seen a horse in my life, much less one at a racetrack.

Suddenly I miss my dad. Why does he have to shave and go to the bank anyway? Hasn't he heard of online banking? The entire routine at the store has been uprooted with Mom being here and talking to Miles about things I don't know about. I look at the clipboard on the counter to find the next order: one packet of fennel seeds—House of Chaat. "I'll be back," I say.

When I get there, I see a huge sign on the wall: "Ready to Eat! Ready to Cook! Come home to House of Chaat!" In the back there are now two refrigerators and a swarm of people around them. How can they have two and we barely have one?

I go past the line and right into the kitchen like I normally do. This time Juhi is at the stove, where the deep fryer is set up.

"Lots of people out there," I say. Of course, there's always lots of people. I don't know why I say that. I want to ask her about the two refrigerators, but at the same time I don't want to hear that House of Chaat is killing it.

"I'm making pakoras," Juhi says. "Want one?"

I watch as she dips a basket of chickpea-battered vegetables into a vat of frying oil. Her hair is up in a net, but there are thin wisps coming out as usual.

"I thought you weren't supposed to," I say.

"Why? I can cook."

"No, fry stuff in the oil. Because of your uncle. Because of, you know . . ." And then instead of finishing the sentence, I reach up to touch her hair, like she touched mine. I have never done this before. It's more like touching a fishing net, but it's still her. I'm touching Juhi Shah's hair, something I've wanted to do since kindergarten.

Juhi's mouth twitches. "I know what I'm doing," she says. She lifts the basket out and empties the chickpea fritters into a tray. She gives me one with a gloved hand and takes one with her other hand that isn't gloved. "It's good, isn't it?" she says as we chew.

I nod, watching her. Around us the kitchen clangs and bangs, voices ringing in the air in English and Hindi, while we stand together like we're on our own island. We use the same napkin to wipe spots of grease from our fingertips and our fingers touch, and it makes me so afraid I don't know what to do. It feels like there are great tectonic shifts happening, that the ground is moving beneath our feet. The only thing that is the same is Juhi's hair. So soft and straight and perfect, even inside a hairnet. Then there's me. But even I'm changing, too. The play has been changing me.

Juhi gets out the money box.

"I'm so ready for summer to be over," she whispers.

I finished swallowing. "Me, too," I whisper back, even though I wish the summer would never end. I want to tell her how the grocery store is failing and my dad has stopped coming to work, and how I'm worried everything is changing too fast. But of course I can't.

"We should do something," she whispers.

My heart quickens. What does she mean? Like a date? Like seeing a movie? I imagine us together in the dark of the theater, our faces lit up from the flashing screen.

"Yeah, we could go somewhere," I offer. Can I do it? Ask her out? Nitya will never believe it.

Before Juhi can respond, Satish Uncle shows up. "Juhi! Customers are waiting for the pakoras. What are you doing gabbing like this?" He snaps his finger at someone else. "Pradeep, come over—see how she's left the fryer unattended."

"I'm right here!" Juhi exclaims. "I'm paying Karthik his money."

Satish Shah nods at me. "Beta, sorry Juhi can't talk to you now, but you are the lifesaver. Tell your daddy that, okay? Satish Shah owes his success to the grocery store around the corner!"

"Sure, okay," I say reluctantly. Being around Satish Shah makes me think of my dad, and not in a good way. Besides, I was just about to do something big and Satish Shah had to ruin it.

As I leave, I glance at Juhi to see if she feels the same way. *We could go somewhere!* But she doesn't look up. She's arranging the pakoras on the tray, and she's glaring. There's something else going on inside her, a storm brewing silently.

EVERYTHING THAT'S CHANGED SINCE SCHOOL GOT OUT

- Dad stopped coming to work.
- Aasif got fired.
- Mom bosses me at the store instead.
- Nitya is under a niceness spell.
- Mrs. R and Mr. J aren't so bad.
- I'm acting in a play!!!
- I'm more like Lenny (minus the hair gel).
- Juhi likes me, but I'm not sure how much.
- I'm happy and worried and scared.

Chapter 31

That night, after Mom and Dad go to bed, Nitya and I sit on the couch playing Battleship and eating mint chip ice cream. It was Nitya's idea. On a break from studying for the SAT this afternoon, she walked down to Star Market and bought a pint of Breyers for us.

We talk about Dad not going to the store the last two days.

"You're home, what does he do?" I ask.

"I'm not sure because I usually sleep in until lunch," Nitya says.

"Great. I'm delivering groceries and you're drooling into your pillow."

She shrugs. "You try staying up all night studying." She dives her spoon into the ice cream.

"Well, whatever he's doing, he's leaving me and Mom to deal with the store."

"How bad can it be? Mom's there."

"Um."

Nitya laughs. "Oh, yeah, right."

I eat a spoon of mint chip. There's something else on my mind. "Did you mean what you said the other day to Raj?"

"What did I say?"

"You know . . . about Indian girls not wanting to date Indian guys?"

"Oh, that." She stops. "You want to ask Juhi out?"

Argh. How does she do that? Guess everything? I wasn't even talking about Juhi.

"Don't worry, Karthu. You're different. You're not a jerk like Raj."

"That's it? We're jerks?"

"No, of course not."

"Then what is it? What's wrong with Indian guys?"

Nitya sweeps up her hair in a bun, twisting a rubber band again and again with her short fingers. "Honestly, I'm not sure. Because when I think of you, Karthu, I don't feel that way. Maybe it's not a problem with all the guys."

"Or it's because you're racist?"

"You keep saying that. I'm Indian. How can I be racist against other Indians?"

"Well, you'd better figure that out, Miss I-want-to-be-a-lawyer."

"What does that have to do with it?" She thinks for a moment. "Have you ever been on the T and there's another Indian sitting across from you? You both know the other person is there, but you don't make eye contact."

"Like you pretend they aren't there."

"Right."

"Mom always says hi," I point out.

"That's because she's Mom. But us. We don't say hi. What's up with that?"

I shrug. The world is full of Indians. Short, tall, skinny, fat, weird, old, young, shy, in your face, looking for discounts at the store, taking the T home. I couldn't possibly talk to all of them. But now that I think of it, I don't talk to *any* of them. Except at the store, but that's only because I'm supposed to. "Doesn't everyone not say hi? Doesn't everyone pretend not to see somebody because . . . ?" Then I stop because I don't know the reason either.

"Maybe it's because we see ourselves in the other person and *we're* the ones that we hate."

"That's deep."

"Isn't it?" She sticks a peg on her board. "And I just sunk your battleship."

Nitya and I play Battleship until midnight. Then we call it quits, and she follows me to my room because she wants her iPod back for the night. She wants to see if listening to music will relax her. "I'm so worried about the SAT. High school is the worst, Karthu. I'm warning you."

"You'll be fine," I say.

I reach under my bed where I'd left the iPod.

"What's that?" Nitya pulls out the play, and I can't believe I didn't hide it somewhere else after Mom found the Bernstein book. But I'm a twit. Maybe that's why no one will date me.

I pivot on my heel. "Give me that."

"*Being Lenny—A Play in One Act by Shanthi Ananth.* What is this?"

"Nothing. It's a play she wrote. She's a customer at the store."

"And she just gave it to you? What gives?" She leans back against my bed and turns the page. "Is this the playwriting student Mom and Dad were talking about?"

"Yes. Now can you give it back to me?"

Nitya flips through the book. "It's about Leonard Bernstein. No wonder you're suddenly into *West Side Story*." She looks at me curiously. "Why so touchy? Did you steal this?"

"No! I just don't want you to damage it."

"Damage it!" Nitya grins. I keep asking for the script, and she gets more and more annoying, waving it in the air away from me, until I want to smack her.

"Give it to me!" I lunge forward and grab the pages out of her hand, which sends her falling backward.

"Oof!" she gasps. Then after a moment, she starts laughing.

I watch her. "You're weird."

She bends over, still laughing. "I haven't seen you that mad before."

"I'm glad I'm so entertaining."

"I don't know why you have Shanthi Ananth's play. Maybe she gives copies of her play to everyone at the grocery store. Or who knows, you're the star of her play, and—" She sees my face. I can't help it. I'm shocked she guessed correctly. "You mean . . . ?"

I lean forward. "You can't tell Mom and Dad. It just happened one day."

Nitya rests against the bed. "What's wrong with them knowing?"

"Dad will freak out about delivering the groceries on time. And don't get me started on Mom."

"She'd tell you it was a waste of time," Nitya guesses.

"All summer long."

She sighs. "You can't let them stop you, Karthu. Remember what I said? We have to be actively rebelling every single minute."

"I don't want to rebel," I say. "I just want this one thing."

"Whatever it is, you have to fight, Karthu," she says. Nitya tries to fake-punch me, but I move out of the way. Someday she'll be a lawyer or a boxer. Or both.

Chapter 32

In the morning, my mom is in the kitchen by herself, drinking coffee.

"Where's Dad?" I ask. "Is he going to the store today?"

Mom sets her coffee cup down. "Your daddy needs a little rest this morning. Come, get ready and we can go together on the T."

My dad needs rest? Since when? For a moment I wonder if he's even in the apartment. Maybe he snuck off to the store without telling anyone. It's hard to believe he missed the past two days. But a third?

Then, after breakfast, we're in the living room putting on our shoes when Dad comes in fully dressed. "It's okay—I'll go to the store. You can stay home," he tells Mom.

Mom is sitting on the couch tying her shoe. "You said you were resting."

"I'm done," he says.

"Take the day off, Manjesh," Mom says. "It's a difficult choice."

Choice? I stop where I am near the front door.

"No, it's not," Dad says.

"It is." Mom is tying her shoe slowly so it's like she's talking to the shoe, not him.

Choice between what?

"But isn't this what you want? I see you at the bulletin board, always adding up things, remembering things, not saying anything, but I know."

Mom watches him wearily, her shoe finally tied. She's wearing Nike tennis shoes and a sundress. A combination of practicality and failed fashion sense.

Then Dad actually starts shouting. "Now we can think about that house in Newton!"

There are exactly three times I've heard my dad shout in my life: when I shorted the microwave by heating up socks, when Nitya bleached the ends of her hair in the bathroom without telling anyone (and bleached the countertop, too). And now.

Mom's voice wavers. "Not like this, Manjesh."

Meanwhile, I'm rooted to the floor. My parents fight all the time. But they never actually disagree. It's the weirdest kind of fighting there is, if you think about it. But this isn't about getting the oil changed in the car or taking out the trash.

"Well, I go to the store every day and I know," Dad goes on. "Masala Max closed. The auto shop closed. Miller is closing."

Mom looks surprised. "The deli guy next door? But he was there yesterday. Lots of sale ads in his window."

"He's moving to Florida. Early retirement. One by one, Roopa, everyone around me is closing down. And then this week, those chairs and cubicles and the endless carpeting . . ."

"Brings back bad memories, I know . . ." Mom murmurs.

"It was GREAT," Dad shouts again. "To go someplace where someone else is thinking about the bottom line for a change." He sinks on the couch, his face in his hands.

"Manjesh, Manjesh . . ." Mom whispers.

Across the living room, I see Nitya in her bathrobe.

What's going on? she mouths to me.

I don't know, I mouth back.

There's a scene in *West Side Story* when Maria repeats Tony's name. "Tony, Tony," she sings. They're singing about their last night together. They don't know it yet, but the audience knows. I feel like the audience now. I don't know what my parents mean by Newton or the endless carpeting, but watching them now in the living room, I know this is a last I'm seeing.

♪

My dad stays back and my mom and I go to the store without him. On the way to the T, and even on the ride to our stop, we don't say anything. It's only when we're walking to the store from the T stop that my mom finally speaks. "You know, your father has worked very hard. The store, he built it from the ground up."

"I thought you hated the store."

She looks at me, hurt. "Hate? How could I hate it? That's like hating your father." We walk past House of Chaat and the line out front, which is now just a normal thing. "I don't know what's so great about them. I tried the potato tikki. Just average. Too much garam masala. You can tell their spices aren't fresh, just store-bought." Which is ironic since a lot of those spices come from our store.

"Then what's going on? Was Dad really at the bank? Are you buying a house in Newton?"

"No, Cutie. There's no house in Newton. But . . ." We cross the street, waiting for a sports car to finish cutting in front of us, roaring like a clown who can go only two miles an hour on Comm Ave.

"But what?"

"I would say expect some changes."

"Like what?" I wave my arms, exasperated. I remember what Nitya said last night, about how we needed to rebel, how we needed to fight. This was why. Because we're powerless. "No wonder Nitya gets pissed off all the time. No one gives a straight answer."

Mom gives me a pained look. "Be patient, Cutie. I'm still trying to figure things out."

We get to the store and for the first time, there's a line at the door. It's Mrs. Carmichael, Mrs. Rodrigues, and Miles.

"No one picked up the phone, so I came," Mrs. Rodrigues says. "Is everything okay? We need two extra-ripe mangos."

"Dude, what gives?" Miles has already started the crossword, which he's holding in his hands.

"Do you know what a late start is, Mr. Miles?" Mom asks.

"Starting later than you're supposed to," he says.

Mrs. Carmichael doesn't say anything until we all get inside, and then she asks if the shipment of frozen multigrain samosas have come in and I tell her yes, they came in yesterday.

Then Mrs. Carmichael says, "What would we do without this place?"

"Yes," Mrs. Rodrigues says, nodding vigorously. "Yes, what would we do without you?"

"Should I turn the sign to open?" I ask, and my mom tells me yes.

Chapter 33

The rest of the week goes by in a blur. I don't have time to think about my parents, because the dress rehearsal is coming up and I'm super nervous. Now Binh knows about the play, too. When I see him on my way to deliver roasted methi powder to House of Chaat, he waves from across the street. "Friday afternoon, count on me," he calls out.

Every day, Juhi tells me how she plans to be at my dress rehearsal, and do I need anything because she and Asha have tons of hair spray and gel. I tell her, "Um, no, I'm good."

Miles doesn't say much except that his mom wanted him to come in for a fluoride rinse on Friday. He told her he couldn't because he was busy. "Dodged *that* bullet," he says.

Part of me is excited, part of me wants it done already. Either way, it's so hard to think of anything other than the play that I feel like I'm out of brain space. And then there's Lenny—thinking about him, dreaming about him—how much Lenny can I be?

Nitya was reading through my lines with me for a while, but now she's not talking to anyone. She says she has to study for the SAT all the time or how else will she get into college. She eats dinner in her room with the door closed.

Meanwhile, Dad is back in the store, and he's decided to have a massive sale. There are all kinds of Buy One Get One Free deals floating through the store for rice and chapatti flour and frozen food. Maybe he got the idea from the deli next door. Mr. Miller has been having those kinds of sales all month.

Thursday afternoon, I run into Binh at his restaurant. "Done with ESL!" he tells me. "My mom told me to celebrate with my good friends. She says take them out for ice cream." He produces a crisp ten-dollar bill from his pocket. I haven't been there in a long time, but with Binh offering to treat, I can't say no.

We don't know where Miles is, so it's just the two of us. We cross the street. The August sky is hazy in that way that only the end of summer can be. I smell popcorn and peanuts and car exhaust in the air. On the other side of the street, we run into Juhi, who's helping load boxes onto the bikes.

"Wait up, I'll join you," she says. "They'll think I'm out with the deliveries."

The three of us walk together, taking up the whole sidewalk. Juhi walks next to me, and every now and then I feel the bump of her shoulder against mine. She's making jokes about the play, how the next one should be called *Being Karthik*.

"Yeah, first scene, Karthik is on his bike," Binh says.

"Second scene, he's eating two scoops of ice cream on a cone," Juhi adds.

Binh shakes his head. "Karthik doesn't eat on a cone."

"Fine, in a bowl. He's almost done then his dad calls. Cut!" Juhi teases.

"Ha ha," I say. "Story of my life."

At the ice cream shop, Juhi sits down on the bench out front. She tells us to go on without her. She has a rock or something in her shoe, and she wants to get it out. So Binh and I go inside, where there are a million people. Where did they all come from? Maybe everyone is feeling the last days of summer, too. Binh and I know already what we want from the menu, but the line is moving slowly and we have to wait. So Binh takes out a pen and draws a skater boy on a napkin that he got from the counter.

"What happened to the space alien with the extra brain?" I ask.

"You remember that?" Binh asks. "That was a while ago."

"I remember everything," I say.

"Yes! This is the same alien boy. The girl didn't want the brain."

"No surprise."

"Yes. He sold it in the black market to buy this high-tech skateboard. He is a big shot now."

I watch Binh add lightning bolts behind the wheels on the skateboard. I can't believe how he does that. Like he doesn't even seem to try hard and his drawings are so good. Though I know Binh draws all the time. He works hard but he doesn't complain. Watching him now, that faint smile on his face, I realize something else.

"You just made up that stuff now, didn't you?"

"Yes." His smile widens. "That's why I like comics."

At the counter, Binh orders a plain vanilla cone. I order a cone, too, just to show I can. Dark chocolate. It's already dripping as I leave the shop. It drips on my finger. I slurp the ice cream from the bottom. I should've gotten a bowl.

When we get back outside, we go to ask Juhi if she wants anything, but now she's not alone. On one side of her on the bench sits Sara Rimsky. On the other side is Jacob Donnell. Sara is laughing at something probably pointless like she always is, but when she sees us, she stops laughing and jumps up. She mumbles something, but no one can hear what she's saying. Meanwhile, Juhi is staring down at her hands. Her back is straight and stiff.

"Kar-dick," Jacob says easily. "What do you call someone who gets stuck in a car?"

"A stud," I say. I look at Juhi, who's twisting the end of her shirt around her finger.

Jacob snorts. "What do you call a car that won't start?"

"Not funny," Binh says.

Jacob shifts back, his arm hanging on the bench behind Juhi. "Juhi is laughing, right?" He nudges her.

"I'm laughing," Sara says, then stops when Binh looks at her.

"It's not funny, Sara," he tells her.

She clears her throat. "Right," she says.

Meanwhile, Juhi still won't look at me. Jacob's arm moves so that his fingers are touching Juhi's arm. He's touching her. *He's touching her.*

"Well, this is getting old," Sara says. "Catch you guys later."

She and Binh exchange looks, and he says, "We will talk later, okay?"

About what? But I don't have time to figure out what Binh means. Meanwhile, Jacob's arm is now resting so easily across Juhi's shoulders. "Hey, Juhi, you should come tomorrow with me and Hoodie," he tells her. "This band my brother knows is playing at the Hatch Shell."

"Um, sure," she says. "Tomorrow night?"

"Nah, earlier. Like afternoon. I'll check with my brother. They need people to show up, you know, cause they're starting out. Even Kar-dick here can come," he says, laughing like a moron.

I ignore him. I've had enough. "Let's go, Binh," I say. "I've got stuff to do."

"Yeah. No time for bad jokers," he says, glaring at Jacob.

As we walk away, Juhi says in a small voice, "Bye, Karthik." That's all she says. No mention of the rehearsal or how she'll be there, even though she's been saying that all week.

My face is burning. Tomorrow afternoon? That's when my dress rehearsal is. She wouldn't ditch it to see some loser band at the Hatch Shell. Would she?

By the time Binh and I get to Harvard Ave, our cones are a mess, dripping over everything. There are splats of vanilla and dark chocolate trailing behind us on the sidewalk.

"Oh boy, these cones are sucking," Binh says seriously. He's using the napkin with the skater alien boy to wipe his fingers.

I'm still thinking what a loser I am for believing anything had changed.

Binh glances at me. "Do not worry about the . . . cones. Know what I mean?"

Around us there is a symphony of car horns.

I nod. "Yeah, Binh. No more cones."

HOW TO GET READY FOR FRIDAY

- Practice your lines in the shower.
- Sing songs from *West Side Story* (I mean, why not?).
- Try the hair gel again and fail.
- Fake-play the piano on your bike handles and get weird looks.
- Forget about ice cream and sucky bands that will suck at the Hatch Shell.

Chapter 34

Now the thought of Friday is excruciating. It isn't just ice cream cones that suck. So does my life. How will I pull off a dress rehearsal with all the suckiness going on?

Nitya continues to eat her meals inside her room. There is a stack of dirty dishes piled up outside her door. Mom would normally hit the roof. But strangely, my parents are being surprisingly nice and no one says anything. My mom and dad seem busy, looking distracted and talking late at night. Something is going on. I would ask Nitya except that she's cloistered herself with her SAT books.

"How come the mangos are reduced price?" Mrs. Rodrigues asks me Friday morning. "That's never happened." I have no answer for her. Maybe my dad has hatched some last-ditch plan to increase our sales and save the store? Or he's trying to get rid of the mangos?

Shanthi notices the Fanta is on sale, too.

"Buy one Fanta get one free—that's awesome!" she says when I bring her a bag of Indian groceries later that morning. She holds up a flyer. "Do you like it? I'm putting it up on campus. Time to advertise."

I look at the flyer. In the middle it says: BEING LENNY: THE PIANO THAT MADE BERNSTEIN—A PLAY IN ONE ACT BY SHANTHI ANANTH. Then at the bottom: DEBUT PERFORMANCE BY KARTHIK RAGHAVAN.

"My name is on it," I say, surprised.

"I know!"

I've never seen my name on a flyer before. It seems so official, like I could be a real actor. I want a flyer to keep, but I don't want it lying around the apartment where someone might see it.

Later that afternoon before the dress rehearsal, I check up on Mr. Jain. He hasn't ordered anything in the last few days. When I buzz his door, he's surprised to see me. "I'm fine, Karthik. But you are a very good boy to inquire." He shows me his foot proudly. The cast is gone and now he's wearing a boot. He can walk around slowly in the apartment and doesn't need crutches. "Come, let me get you some tea."

"Um, I have to go soon and—"

"It's iced tea. It's already made."

"Well, okay. I can get it . . ."

But Mr. Jain won't have any of that. He makes me sit down, and he even gives me the crossword, which he's mostly finished, but he asks if I can fill in the ones he hasn't figured out yet. He disappears into the kitchen. I look around. The apartment is cleaner. There's even a vase of fresh flowers near the window. I wonder if his daughter brought it, or if Mr. Jain got it now that he can walk with his boot.

He comes out with a stainless steel tumbler of iced tea and a plate of Parle-G biscuits. Oh, man. I mentally calculate how long it will take me to consume all of that. I'm supposed to meet Binh and Miles at the corner of Harvard and Chester in fifteen minutes so we can go together to Shanthi's place. I have no idea what Juhi's doing. I haven't seen her since yesterday.

I don't want to be late meeting Binh and Miles, so I eat fast, stuffing my mouth with biscuits one after another. Mr. Jain talks the entire time. He talks about how Australia was lucky to win the World Cup two years ago and how they can't possibly win the next one with all the cricket players India has lined up. He says India's time to shine is coming. "We all have our moment to shine," Mr. Jain says.

"Gotta go, Mr. J," I say after I chug the last of my iced tea.

It wasn't that bad. It was sweet and there was a hint of mint. I can still taste it in my mouth when I'm outside.

♪

Binh, Miles, and I get to Shanthi's apartment on time. No one brings up Juhi. Maybe Binh told Miles about yesterday. Or maybe Miles forgot that Juhi was supposed to be here. The only person who mentions anything is Shanthi.

"Hey guys," she says when she sees us. She looks behind me and says, "What about . . ."

But I shake my head quickly and that's all that's said.

Inside, Shanthi has transformed her apartment. She pushed aside furniture and used colored tape to mark out the stage area. She's also hung up black curtains across the wall behind it to make a dark backdrop and arranged the dining chairs in a row. There are three chairs. Miles and Binh sit down in two of them, and the third one is left empty.

A few minutes later, the buzzer buzzes again and it's Ezra and Amanda. They smile at me.

"It's Lenny," Amanda says.

"For twenty-one minutes," I say.

Shanthi makes a final adjustment to the track lights and announces the play. "*Being Lenny—The Piano That Made Bernstein—A Play in One Act by Shanthi Ananth*. That's me. The roles of Sam and Jeannie Bernstein will be played by Ezra Katz and Amanda Hathaway. The role of Lenny will be played by Karthik Raghavan."

Miles and Binh clap and Miles says, "Woot woot," which is kind of silly but nice. The lights dim except for the stage, and we begin.

At first it's hard for me to get into it. It helps that the lights are focused on me and that Amanda and Ezra are playing the other parts. But it feels like we're all reading lines, not acting, and the empty third chair is distracting me. My mind wanders, and I wonder if Juhi is at the Hatch Shell with Jacob, if she remembers that the rehearsal is now. Of course she does. Which only makes it worse.

I catch Shanthi's eyes. She's watching me quizzically and gently. She senses that I'm not all there. I swallow. What did she tell me before? The audience is there to give you energy. I'm supposed to draw my energy from them.

"It's not every day a piano shows up in your apartment," I tell Miles and Binh. And I remember how acting isn't just about your lines and the props you use. It's about the audience, too.

So I concentrate on my friends. On Miles, who's walked home with me every day since third grade when he first moved to Allston, and how he might have to move again depending on what happens to his dad. And Binh, who always serves me soup in his family's restaurant, who told me not to worry about cones dripping on us. And Shanthi, who saw me as an actor from day one. I try to imagine I'm telling them the story of Lenny and who he was when he was young. Who gets a piano sent to them? Lenny does. But what do his parents do? Not understand. Not see the piano for what it is: the beginning.

I try to show all of that with my face and my body and my voice. The lines keep coming and it's like I'm a fountain of words. This is the gift I'm giving in the darkened room, with black curtains and track lighting. I imagine that in telling the story of Lenny, I'm telling the story of myself, of Miles and Binh, and Shanthi, too. We are all waiting for the piano to arrive. We are all waiting for our lives to begin.

Chapter 35

I wake up the next morning to an empty apartment. On the dining table, I find an article and an apple with a note under it that says: *Cutie, Took Nitya to SAT. Daddy is at the store. He says even though it's Saturday, stay home and enjoy your day off. Love, Mom. p.s. I left you an article on exocytosis. Tell me what you think.* I look at the article cut out from *Science*. Who reads about exo-whatever on their day off? Instead, I spread out on the couch and watch *Star Trek* episodes back-to-back.

The play rehearsal went pretty well yesterday. It helped that Amanda and Ezra did the other parts, because I got to practice the timing—like knowing when to say things. The space around the lines, how long you have to wait between people speaking, is longer than you'd think. But most of all, I'm glad Miles and Binh were there. The energy *was* different. I had to talk louder, more clearly, and fill up the room. I had to feel people breathing. The whole time, though, I hated seeing the empty chair. It was like having Juhi there, but also a reminder that she wasn't.

I must have fallen asleep on the couch, because the next thing I know, the front lock opens and it's Nitya and my parents. I rub my eyes. "What time is it?"

"What, sleeping all day, Cutie?" Mom asks. "It's two o'clock."

"I am sooooo happy to be done!" Nitya says, throwing her arms out like she's embracing the world. "Karthik can have all my SAT books."

"Um, no thanks," I say. "Why is Dad home already?"

Mom and Dad look at each other.

"We have to talk," he says to Nitya and me.

She flops next to me. "Uh-oh. I hope it isn't bad news, because I'm having a good day."

"It's wonderful news," Mom says. "You can keep having a good day."

Dad sits down on the chair across from Nitya and me while Mom stands next to him, her back straight like an invisible wall pressing against her. Something about the way she stands makes me think they've rehearsed what he's going to say, and even where she'll be in the room when he's talking. Shanthi calls it blocking. She says actors plan how they're going to move, along with what they're going to say.

Dad rests his hands on his knees. "So, kids. I got a computer job."

Nitya sits up. "Whoa."

"I'm lucky," he says. "After years of being out of the industry, I found a way back in. When everybody else is getting laid off, I'm getting hired."

"Daddy is very lucky," Mom says. "These things don't always happen."

"But I thought you hated computers," I say, surprised.

He shakes his head. "No, I just hated working for someone else. It was good being away. Creating something with my own hands."

"It's a very good store," Mom says.

"It was a very good store," Dad corrects her. "Was."

"You mean we're closing?" I ask. What are my parents talking about? This is terrible news. How will the Mrs. Rodrigueses manage without me bringing them mangos every day? How will Mr. Jain get his tea and snacks when he still has a week with his boot, and then who knows, weeks of physical therapy afterward?

"Where did you get this job suddenly?" Nitya asks. "When did you even interview?"

I remember the conversation from a few days ago. "Is this job in Newton?"

"Newton!" Nitya shrieks. "Are we moving?"

"Not Newton, Baby," Mom says. "It's Pavan Uncle's company."

"You mean he just gave Daddy a job?" Nitya crosses her arms. "Isn't that nepotism?"

"He interviewed, didn't he?" I ask. That would explain the shaving, and the shirt and tie on the bed. Mom was in on the whole thing.

"Yes, Cutie," Mom says. "He did interview, and he got a job because he's good."

"But Pavan Uncle works in Worcester," I say. It's like we're back to the beginning of the summer, when my mom wanted my dad to get the job in Worcester. It's like this summer never happened. Except that I wasted my time doing deliveries on Raj's crappy bike.

"So we *are* moving," Nitya wails. "Only it's not to sucky Newton. It's to sucky Worcester. Great, there goes being captain of the debate team this year."

"Baby, not now," Mom says.

"You don't understand," Nitya says, crumpling. "I just took the SAT. I study all the time. Honors this, honors that. Now, finally, it's senior year and I get to be leader of something, and poof, gone."

Mom sighs. "Nothing is decided yet."

Nitya starts to cry. "Daddy, I'm happy for you. Really. But this is the worst news ever for me." Then she gets up and my parents call after her, but she disappears into her room.

"It's a lot to take in," Mom says. "What about you, Cutie? You'll see, this is good for everyone."

I feel like running out of the room, too, but strangely I'm rooted to the couch.

"Why didn't you tell us you were interviewing?" I ask. "That stuff about the bank wasn't true."

"I'm sorry, Karthu," Dad says. "But it was too early to say anything. And Nitya had her SAT. I didn't want to distract her."

"It looks like you distracted her now."

"Cutie." Mom gives me a look.

"You tell us what to do all the time, and when it comes to decisions that affect us, we don't get a say in anything. We don't even get to know until it's too late."

Mom frowns. "Have you seen our financial statements? Have you seen our bills? Do you know how much it costs to send Nitya to college and then, who knows, law school someday. You can't do it on a grocery store paycheck."

"I guess that's why you need me to be a doctor," I say coldly. "To pay your bills."

I know this isn't true, and I don't even believe it, but it's out of my mouth before I can help it. I don't want to move to Worcester, and I don't want the store to be over. It's all happening too fast.

Mom's eyes get small and hard. "That is *not* the reason you should be a doctor," she says fiercely. "I just think it's the best profession in the world, something honorable. You have the chance, I didn't. You are so lucky, Cutie."

"If you love it so much, why don't *you* be one?"

"Don't be ridiculous."

I look at her. Really look at her. There are fine lines around her eyes, and she has maybe the worst fashion sense I've seen in my life, though I'm the last person to have an opinion on that. But I see something else, and maybe it's because I've been acting that I can imagine other lives. "You're about the same age Leonard Bernstein was when he wrote *West Side Story*," I tell her. "You always tell us to do what we're good at. You took care of Miles when he got a glass splinter at the store."

"What?" Dad asks.

Mom shakes her head. "That was nothing."

"You know about the heart," I go on. "You've always wanted to be a doctor. *You're* the one who should go to med school." I'm not sure what I'm doing, but suddenly it feels right.

"Cutie, drop it," she says.

"Roopa." Dad looks thoughtful and reflective, like when he's concluded that whole-grain atta flour is a good product to stock in the store. "I think . . . Karthu is onto something."

Mom has the biggest shocked look on her face. "Me?" Her voice goes up at the end like the last bar of a Shostakovich piano concerto.

The room is quiet. In the distance, we can hear muffled crying.

"I should go check on Nitya," Mom murmurs.

"I think she would probably kill you," I say.

"Roopa," Dad repeats. "Listen to what Karthu says."

"I can handle Baby," Mom says.

"Not about Nitya. About you. Why didn't we think of this before? I start a new job and you go back to school."

"Are you serious?" she asks. "You really think I can?"

But now that the idea has taken hold, she and dad can't stop talking. They think about all the possibilities, like where she could take premed classes for cheap, like UMass Boston, because the tuition is in-state.

"Think, we might have two doctors in the family someday," Mom says, smiling at me.

"Um . . ." Before I can say more, Nitya returns, perhaps to give my parents a second round of admonishment. Instead, she discovers something else. A new plan hatching.

"Mom," she asks incredulously, "wants to go to med school?"

"Out of this world, I know," Mom says, her face flushed. "But I'm really thinking about what Cutie said. How I always wanted to study the heart. And take charge of my own life and . . ." Her voice breaks. "I didn't think I ever had a chance. And now Cutie is telling me these things, and isn't that what I've been telling you both all along? To know what you want and go for it?"

"Right," I say slowly. I'm kind of zonked she's even listening to me.

"I don't know why the dweeb gets all the credit," Nitya says to Mom. "You're the one who wants to be a doctor."

"Well, let's see how that goes. First I've got to take the premed classes. Then the MCAT."

This is when Mom and Dad decide that if she's going to take classes in Boston, it will be easier to stay in Allston. Also, we'll have to save money for when Nitya goes to college and Mom goes to med school.

"So we're *not* moving!" Nitya cries. "Hurray for Mom! This is so freaking cool!"

"There are no guarantees," Mom says. But her eyes are shining.

"Only hope," Dad adds.

Everyone starts talking at once, happy and relieved. Dad says he has to sign the contract and maybe he'll start his new job in September. Mom has to enroll in organic chemistry. Meanwhile, there's the store. The lease ends September 15. We will have to be moved out by then.

By the time we're done, it's midnight. Mom goes off to bed and Nitya does, too. Dad says he's coming. By now, he's sitting on the couch, and in his hand he has the crossword, something he never does, but he's looking at it intently, trying to fill in the blank spaces.

I sit down next to him and look over his shoulder. "Sopranos, eight down," I tell him. "Haven't you heard of the show?"

"What, have you?" he asks. I watch him count the boxes with his pencil tip.

"Did you really want the job, Dad?" No one else seems to remember about the store closing except me.

He's still counting.

"It fits, Dad. I know. Just write it in."

He finishes counting and then writes in the word "Sopranos." "Yes, Karthu."

"But why? Didn't you say we have to take chances in life?"

Dad puts down his pencil. "We definitely have to take chances," he tells me. "And I did with the store. I worked hard, and to me, hard work doesn't just lead to success. It *is* success. The store is the accomplishment I am most proud of. Do you know why? Do you know why I started the grocery store in the first place?"

"Because you were fired?"

Dad winces. "You're always so direct, Karthu."

"Sorry."

Dad leans back. "When Mom and I moved to Albuquerque from India, when we were first married, we were so lonely. We had each other, but we knew no one else. And then one day we were at the Indian grocery store and we met our first friend. He was not South Indian, like us. He was from Rajasthan, like Mr. Jain."

"Right," I say. "Mr. J talks a lot about Rajasthan."

Dad nods. "And then we met a family from Delhi, and of course, we met people from South India. And that's when I realized, the grocery store is a place to meet people from all over India—and all around the world. Because food is what we all have in common, no matter what else." He clasps his hands together. "And I wanted to be the one to do that when we came to Boston. To bring people together. My people together."

It's true. At the store, we know people from all over India, like Mr. Jain and Mrs. Rodrigues. We also know people from all over Boston, some who aren't Indian at all.

"Then why give all that away?" I ask quickly. "What about Mr. Jain? He's finally walking. And Mrs. Rodrigues. She needs the mangos for her mother-in-law. And . . ."

"Karthu, I took a chance." Dad quietly unclasps his hands. "But this computer job isn't just about me. It's about our family, too. Nitya has to go to college. And some day, you."

"But . . . but I thought the store was your dream." Before I know it, I'm crying. No one else seems as sad as me. No one else feels the earth moving under our feet. No one else remembers so much, and to remember is to know what's gone. Now Mom is going to med school, Nitya will be off to college, and everyone still thinks I'm going to be a doctor. Meanwhile, I'm stuck with no dream, and my dad just lost his.

I bend over and Dad rests a hand on my shoulder and lets me cry. I feel his rough, callused hand on my arm. The history of our store, all those years, are there in the weight of his hand.

"I loved the store with all my heart," Dad says. "But I had my time, Karthu. It's now time for Mom to shine."

Chapter 36

Mom is shining all right. Every morning, she has a list of things to do at the store. Nitya has been tasked with going to the Barnes & Noble in Kendall Square to get study books for Mom. One for the MCAT, plus prep books for organic chemistry, cell biology, and statistics. I'm in charge of printing out signs at Staples—signs that say EVERYTHING MUST GO, THREE FOR ONE, and the biggest one: AFTER TEN YEARS, WE REGRET TO SAY GOODBYE. After the signs are printed, I see a typo—AFTER TEN TEARS, WE REGRET TO SAY GOODBYE. Mom says it doesn't matter, we will use them anyway.

She and Dad are furiously packing and selling and getting customers to buy everything in the store. It's amazing how much gusto Mom has. Maybe she should have been working here all these years. We sell more than we ever have, and I can hardly keep up with the bagging or delivering.

The first person in the store is Mrs. Carmichael. "I knew it," she says. "As soon as the refrigerator broke, I knew the jig was up."

What jig? She seems devastated by the news. She is buying up bags and bags of whole-grain atta flour and several boxes of multi-grain frozen samosas. "Now I'll have to shop in Brookline," she says reproachfully to my dad. "And everyone knows there's no parking there. This store is just a short walk from my building."

He smiles at her. "Brookline is a lovely place to shop, you'll find," he says.

"Take the T," Mom says unhelpfully. Honestly, if she's going to be a doctor, she needs to learn more people skills.

Mrs. Rodrigues is indignant. "Everyone knows that there is no such thing as a reduced-price mango," she says when I step into her apartment.

"Karthik, I heard the terrible news of your father vacating the store," says the other Mrs. Rodrigues. She's standing in the middle of the room without her walker, and Rani on her shoulder. She's been taking daily walks around the family room with the bird, trying to keep steady so the bird doesn't fly away from her. She says this has done wonders for her coordination and balance. Rani has flown away only twice, perching on one of the curtain rods (I was the one who had to get her down both times). "Before the excellent mango lassis and company, I was so weak," she says to me. "Now both Rani and me, we are liberated."

"My dad got a new job," I explain to them. Rani squawks at me. But I'm used to it now. I don't even flinch. "And my mom is going back to school."

"That's very nice, but how will we replace you?" says the younger Mrs. R. "You're such a clever boy."

"He should tutor the boy next door," says the older Mrs. R. "Don't you think? They're looking for someone."

"But Karthik's moving," Mrs. R tells her mother-in-law. "Didn't you hear him?"

"No, we're just closing the store. I'll be around." I wonder if I should offer to deliver mangos still. But how would that be possible?

The two Mrs. Rodrigueses make me stay a whole hour. I have to eat pineapple cake and look at photos of the older Mrs. Rodrigues when she was young, and photos of the younger Mrs. Rodrigues when she was even younger, some when she wasn't Mrs. Rodrigues yet. There are baby pictures and wedding pictures and pictures of Mr. Rodrigues, whom I've never met. It's weird how much of their lives they're sharing with me now that I'm leaving.

Shanthi comes over to the store as soon as she hears the news.

"Oh my god," she says to my parents and me, "I'm so sorry you're closing. I love the spicy hot chips. No one else carries this kind."

Dad is used to these conversations with the customers. It seems to get easier every time, knowing what to say, but his shoulders seem to sag more each time, too.

"I'm sorry the store is closing, too," he tells her. "We will miss everyone so much."

"When I remember BU and grad school," Shanthi says, "I'll remember the spicy-hot chips and Fanta. Know what I mean?"

Mom watches her curiously. "You're the one who writes plays, yes?"

I'm instantly on high alert. My dad is clueless about most things, but my mom is a hawk. Any moment, Shanthi will say something, she'll mention the play, and I won't be Lenny anymore. But then the miracle happens, which is that Miles and Binh suddenly show up.

"Dude," Miles says. "What's going on? The store's closing?" He looks at all the signs, including the one with the ten tears.

"We are hearing the news only now," Binh says. "My parents say they are very sad. They like your store. They have bought Chinese eggplant and Thai basil, and they like the spicy chips. You are good neighbors, too."

Shanthi smiles at everyone. I get even more panicky—all three of them are congregated in front of my parents. It wouldn't take much to knock down the walls of my carefully guarded secret. But to my surprise, Shanthi quietly slips out the door. "See you later," she says softly to me as she leaves.

Miles and my mom are talking, all about med school and how Miles's mom said her decision to study dental hygiene was the best she'd ever made. "Except, like no one can find their laundry anymore," he says. "And I have to floss. But, uh, I guess she's happy."

Binh nods. "No family likes change. But it happens."

"Why don't you boys have some frozen mango bars?" Mom says. "Take a break, Cutie."

Binh raises an eyebrow. I guess he's never heard my mom's humiliating nickname for her second-born. We all help ourselves to frozen bars and sit outside on the curb away from my family.

"Did you know this was going to happen?" Miles asks. He's the first to unpeel his bar.

"No," I tell him. "My dad interviewed without telling us. And I never thought my mom would go back to school. It all worked out, and I'm glad we're not moving to Worcester."

Miles pushes up his glasses with his free hand. The redness from his sunburn has gone from his face and now he just looks tan with some color in his cheeks. He's wearing a blue polo shirt and khaki shorts, and for the first time he's starting to look like a high school student.

"Speaking of moving," he says. "I am."

We both look at him.

"My dad's not going to be a plumber anymore. He's going into sales for a heating and cooling company in Weymouth."

"Weymouth," I repeat.

"Yeah, about an hour from here. He says he can work normal hours, and my mom can start working in a year. First he thought he'd commute, but Mom wants all of us together now that Spencer's going away to college. They think it's better to move before I start high school. I mean, technically, high school starts in two weeks. So we have to move, like, now."

I'm trying to digest this news, even though Miles had basically warned me already. Here I was worrying I might move to Worcester when my best friend is moving instead.

"You are okay with the moving?" Binh asks.

"No, it sucks," Miles says. "I don't want to start high school somewhere else. I won't know anyone."

"Yes, neither will I," Binh says quietly.

We look at him quickly. "Wait, you too?" I ask.

He nods. "It is, what do you say? Last minute? Unexpected. In the spring, I applied to a private school in Cambridge. But I did not get in. They were concerned about my English proficiency. I was on waiting list. All summer I did ESL. I did not hope too much. I am happy in Allston. My friends are here. My friends and . . ." He stops, flushing.

Who else, I wonder, but Binh goes on. "Last week, all of sudden, we hear I am accepted," he says. "We are conflicted. It is a lot of money. We were prepared for that before. Now, we are not sure. Too much going on. But my parents think I should go."

"Well, do you want to go?" Miles asks.

"Do you get to choose?" I ask.

Binh shrugs. "I think I have to go," he says.

Meanwhile, I suck on the last of my frozen mango bar. I survey the school year ahead of me. Miles, my best friend since third grade, moving. Binh, the only other person I really like, also leaving. Juhi, the girl I've liked since kindergarten, still here, and dissing me. Jacob, Hoodie, Sara, still around to give me grief. Maybe I was better off moving to Worcester.

Behind us, Mom walks by. "Cutie, I'm going to BU for a short while," she says. "I want to check out a few things at the registrar's office. I will be back soon." She stops, seeing my long face, and it's on the tip of her tongue to ask what's wrong, but then she glances at Miles and Binh and seems to change her mind. "Some serious friend talk going on here, right? Don't mind me."

We all kind of hem and haw, squinting at her in the sun. We don't say much else until she's gone.

Miles says, "She doesn't know about the play, does she?"

Binh looks at me. "It is a secret? Karthik, you know what happens to people with secrets."

Miles pretends to get stabbed in the chest.

Binh pretends to get choked.

I crumple up the empty wrapper in my hand. I can't think of what to say in response.

♪

About an hour later, I'm in the store helping Dad take down a shelf in the back. We're disassembling the bolts when we hear the door open and close. We both think it's a customer. But it's Mom. She walks over to us. She has a flyer in her hand.

"We have enough flyers, don't you think?" Dad asks her.

She holds it up. "This isn't ours. Look at this one. Hanging up in the registrar's office at BU."

As soon as I see it, I groan inwardly. Of course. I should have known that one of Shanthi's flyers would make its way into my mom's hands. Just an hour ago, Binh told me I would get caught. How can he be right so soon?

"*Being Lenny: The Piano That Made Bernstein—A Play in One Act by Shanthi Ananth*," Dad reads. "Oh, the girl who was in the store earlier."

"Read the bottom," Mom says. "Look what it says." Then she reads it out loud for him. "Debut performance by Karthik Raghavan."

Dad and Mom look at me like I'm a bug in a science experiment that has suddenly sprouted an extra set of wings. Then Dad asks, "Is this you, Karthu?"

Chapter 37

"Of course, it's him," Mom says. "It makes sense. Why else was he talking about Bernstein?"

Dad blinks. It's obvious he can't keep up with the speed of my mom's brain. Meanwhile, Mom has already pieced together everything—the Fanta and chips delivery, the library book, and *West Side Story*, which we so casually watched together. I can see it all in her eyes. But what do they add up to in her mind? A waste of time? Lying and scheming? High treason?

"Why, Karthik?" she demands. "Why do this and not tell us?"

"I was going to," I mumble. "Just didn't get to it."

"Didn't get to it?" Mom repeats. "When were you planning to get to it?"

"Let's not jump the gun," Dad says. "Sounds harmless. She's a nice girl and—"

"It's not harmless," Mom says. "He lied."

My eyes narrow. "I didn't *lie* about anything. Not like you and dad did about his job."

Mom crosses her arms. "We told you, didn't we? When we had all the information. But you've known this for a long time. At the beginning of the summer you were asking, how about piano lessons, Mom? How about acting lessons, Mom?"

"So what?" I feel myself tightening up. This was definitely not the way I'd planned to tell them about the play. But now I think, who cares? My mom would have reacted the same way no matter what.

"So what? Maybe I'd like to have a say in the matter. We know nothing about Shanthi. What if she expects to be paid money?"

"There's no charge to be in her play," I say quietly.

"Okay. Well then why isn't she paying you?"

"Paying me? Are you kidding me? You have no idea what you're talking about!"

"I know enough," Mom retorts.

"Don't you know how hard it is to get into a playwriting program? She's really talented. And she could have cast someone else. They hire professional actors, that's what she told me. But she didn't want someone else. She wanted me."

"You?" Dad asks.

I flush. "Yeah, me." The weight of that bears down on me. She wanted *me*. I was somebody that stood out in a good way. Maybe for the first time in my life.

Dad holds out his hands as if to stop Mom and me from colliding. "So he's in this play, Roopa. We'll ask Shanthi about it. You can invite your friends . . . when is it, again?" He tries to look at the flyer, but Mom holds on to it tight.

"Not know enough, that's what you think," she tells me. "You think I don't know anything." For some reason, that really bugs her. More than me lying.

"You don't know about art and music and what makes people happy," I say savagely.

There's a silence. Mom's face is pinched tight. I can see she can barely get the words out.

She holds up the flyer. "Is this what makes you happy?"

"Well, I don't want to be a doctor!"

We stand there, squaring off. Behind her, the sunlight pools in from the front window, casting shadows along the wall.

Mom hands over the flyer to Dad. "You go if you want, Manjesh. I probably wouldn't understand any of it because what do I know about art and music."

"Roopa—" Dad starts.

"Enough," she cuts him off. "We have work to do. And look, customers."

She goes to greet the person that came in as Dad and I continue dismantling the shelf. We can hear her voice travel unevenly as she tries to chat. "You are here for the two-for-one deals? I bet you are ready for that. You are looking ready to cook-cook, yes?"

Even from where we stand, we can see the customer, a middle-aged woman, is put off by the false note in my mom's voice. "Just looking, thanks. And you don't need to follow me."

Dad and I glance at each other.

Mom sucks as usual.

From then on, my mom gives me the cold shoulder. It starts with little things like not folding my laundered clothes.

"You're old enough to fold your own clothes," she says, leaving them in a heap on my bed.

Then she stops making me hot milk with honey at night. She stops making popcorn with chaat powder while I'm watching *Star Trek*. She stops lining up my shoes near the front door so they're ready for me when I leave. Now I find them wherever I last kicked them off, near the couch or under my bed or by the bathroom.

Okay, so that makes me sound like a pig. And fine, my mom doesn't need to do all those things for me. But that's not what I notice the most. It's that she stops talking to me. She stops cutting out articles and asking my opinion. She doesn't want to know if I think there will be another financial crisis, or if global warming is real, or if we should ban flavored cigarettes. It's just silence, in the midst of closing the store, registering for college classes, and buying us school supplies for the first day of school.

Even Nitya notices. "You really pissed her off. I've never seen her this mad."

I sigh. "But I'm not trying to make her mad. I want her to listen to me."

"It's about time someone stood up to her, Karthu."

Is that what this is? Me standing up to her? It doesn't feel that way. Plus, I don't see Nitya standing up to her. Instead they're getting along surprisingly well. She's helping Mom pick out study guides for the MCAT. Then the other night, Mom took a practice MCAT while Nitya timed her and tallied up the results. "Not good. You need to work on your acids and bases."

When Mom looked defeated, Nitya bolstered her up. "Don't worry. When you take chem this fall, you'll learn all of that. I'll help you."

"You got your own studies, Baby. Don't waste your time on me."

"We'll be study buddies," Nitya said. "Stud buds."

"Or stud duds, who knows?" Mom joked and they both laughed.

It was the weirdest thing, seeing them get along.

Meanwhile, I'm glad I told Mom I don't want to be a doctor. But telling her isn't enough. Because she will just try to plan my life some other way. What I really want is to have my own choices, to have the whole world open up for me, the way it did for Lenny. When Mom was growing up, wasn't that what she wanted, too? I just wish there was a way to explain all that to her.

♪

Friday morning, we get an order from House of Chaat. Bay leaves and cinnamon sticks. It's been a week since I last saw Juhi, and that was when she was sitting on the bench with Jacob. She didn't even try to find out how the rehearsal went. Well, who cares now.

As I bike over, I keep thinking how I will act when I see her. In my head, I practice what I'll say: *Oh, yeah, play rehearsal went great, we didn't need you there.* Or if she doesn't ask about the rehearsal, then: *How's it going? Yeah, I've been busy, store's closing.* But it all sounds pathetic. It isn't like learning lines for a play. I guess you can't rehearse life.

When I get to the restaurant, I go to the kitchen. Juhi is packing orders, wearing her usual brown apron and hairnet. Her face is cast down and she looks very serious, like she's concentrating on an important mission. She doesn't look up from her packing.

It's Satish Shah who greets me. He comes and shakes my hand with both of his.

"We heard the news, beta," he says seriously. "Your father is a good man. That grocery store, I know it well. I sourced for him many years, fine reputation."

"Thanks," I say stiffly. Isn't he one of the reasons why my dad is going out of business? Isn't he the shark? But for some reason, he isn't acting like a shark. He isn't even acting like his loud, boisterous self. He looks somber and pensive.

"It won't be the same without him," says Satish Shah. He snaps his fingers. "Juhi, pay him. What are you waiting for? And some samosa chaat, free of charge."

Juhi looks up and feigns surprise, as if she just noticed I'm here. She hurries to the cash box. As she gives me the money, she avoids my eyes. "Is that the right amount?" she asks.

"Yeah," I say.

Satish Shah nudges her. "And the chaat. Don't forget that."

"Yes, Satish Uncle," she says tonelessly.

Satish Shah is about to leave when he turns back. "And remember what I said. No frying the pakoras. I saw you doing that before."

"I know!" Juhi now looks up, her eyes flashing. "You told me ten times today."

"How else do I make you listen?" he says before leaving through the swinging door.

"He's the one who never listens to anybody," Juhi says, glowering. "That's my recipe we're using for the pakoras. I'm the one who ground everything up. I have a brain." She looks at me, waiting for me to respond when she catches herself, as if she remembers then that we aren't speaking.

I wait in silence as she gets the chaat. She bites her lip as she hands the Styrofoam box to me. She seems like she wants to say something, but I'm not going to let her. Mom isn't the only one who can give the silent treatment.

♪

That afternoon, Mr. Jain comes to the store. He's walking with a cane and his foot is still in a boot. He's wearing a different new shirt—it has blue stripes and looks surprisingly nice on him. His face is bright and there's color in his cheeks.

"This boy is very, very good," he tells Mom at the register as she rings up his tea and biscuits. "You are his mother, yes?"

"The one and only," she says.

"He takes good care of me, making me noodles. And good company."

"Oh?" Mom glances at me.

"Your foot better, Mr. J?" I ask.

"Getting there," Mr. Jain says. He takes the bag from Mom. "You are doing good job, raising him. Keep up the good work."

Mom smiles with her eyes crinkling. She's embarrassed and pleased at the same time. Even though she doesn't say anything to me after Mr. Jain leaves.

♪

"She's still not speaking to me," I say as Miles and I eat ice cream cones on Comm Ave. He came to join me on a break from the store and we went to Carmine's. I've switched over to cones even though they're drippy and make a mess. But at least now we can walk and talk outside and there's nothing to throw away.

"Is your mom coming to the play?" he asks me.

I shrug. "She said she wouldn't. But she was mad. I guess she's still mad, though."

Miles slurps the top of his Sloopy-Goopy. "Once my mom didn't talk to me for a week because I told her she looked a toad."

"Like when you were two?"

Miles shakes his head. "Nah, last year. We have to get all dressed up every year for Thanksgiving at my grandma's, and, like, they hate each other, my mom and her. It's this contest between them, who can dress the fanciest and have the nicest table and stuff, and my dad and Uncle Milton are, like, leave us out of it, we'll handle the beer."

"Really?"

"Yeah, then before we go, Mom asks me, 'How do I look? Nobody ever tells me how I look.' So I said she looked like a toad. We were reading about them in science. It was the first thing I thought of."

I laugh. "I remember that unit on amphibians. Toads and newts."

"After a week, she forgot. So will your mom."

I eat my Caramel Swirl cone to the end and lick my sticky fingertips. It's not so bad, this cone thing. Maybe Lenny ate from a cone when he talked to girls and walked on Comm Ave or through Harvard or wherever. Or maybe he didn't eat them because it made his hands too sticky to play the piano. Who knows? I can't do everything like Lenny. Sometimes I have to do things like myself.

I just wish ice cream cones didn't remind me of Juhi.

We're about halfway back to the store from Carmine's when we first start to smell it—a thick, acrid smell like the bonfire I went to at the end of sixth grade. The smell is filling the air around us, and the crowd of people on the sidewalk are commenting on it, too. Miles and I pause as we hear the wail of a fire truck in the distance.

"Something's on fire," Miles says.

"Look at the sky," I say, pointing. There's a plume of smoke ahead of us. Like a barbecue on the rooftop terrace of someone's apartment. One summer, our neighbors had a party on our roof and the grill made lots of smoke from charred patties and corn on the cob. But this isn't a rooftop barbecue.

A sudden fear grips me. It can't be the store, can it? The smoke is coming from over where Comm Ave and Harvard meet. And if Mom and Dad are there, then—

The same fire truck we heard a few seconds ago rushes past us, its siren blaring as it goes by.

"Come on," I say to Miles.

We hurry down Comm Ave until we're a block away and Mr. Miller's deli comes into view. And then the grocery store and the sign in front: AFTER TEN TEARS, WE REGRET TO SAY GOODBYE. Mr. Miller doesn't even have signs. He's already gone. His store is completely empty, and ours will be soon. Still, from where Miles and I are, I can see that Mr. Miller's deli and my dad's store are okay. I start to breathe more easily. But I don't stop until I get there and see my parents inside. Miles and I go in and everyone is talking at the same time.

"Karthik! Miles!" Dad exclaims. "Good. We're hearing fire trucks."

"Yeah, it smells like smoke everywhere," Miles says.

"I wonder what it can be?" Mrs. Carmichael says, worried. Her shopping cart is filled for the third day in a row. She is desperate to stock up before we're gone.

"Can't be good," Mom says grimly. "Let's pray nobody is hurt." Once, she made me read an article about a huge wildfire in California that was started by a ten-year-old boy who lit a match. I wonder if Mom is thinking about that article now.

We hear a second truck go by, which makes everyone talk more. Dad tries to find out on the computer if something has been reported in Allston. Then suddenly the door flies open. It's Binh. He's been running and his face is flushed.

"Karthik, you are here. Must tell you," he gasps. We surround him instantly. Binh's eyes are large, tremendous. He can't catch his breath.

"Are you okay?" I say. "Is it a fire?"

Maybe it's near his restaurant. What if it's his place? We lean forward, as if to buffer him from the terrible news he's about to share.

Binh takes great big breaths. He nods rapidly, his hands stretched out. "You must know, everyone. It is on fire! House of Chaat is on fire!"

Chapter 38

Somehow, I get to Harvard Ave and my parents, Miles, and Binh are behind me. For someone with a good memory, how we got here is blurry. We must have all run. Even Mom and Dad. Though they probably ran to stop me.

The flames are blue orange and I can see them from far away, growing higher and higher as I get closer. The air is dusty with smoke. I can feel it in my eyes and my throat. I've never seen a building on fire. I didn't know that concrete and steel and brick can burn with such heat, and when they do, the smell cuts the air like a knife. It's so hot and bright. My legs start to shake. But I press on, through crowds of people on the sidewalk, everyone talking at once. Some of them are bewildered or curious, their faces like ghosts, eyes raised upward. A few are crying. The smoke is making my eyes tear, and it's hard to know if I'm crying or not, too.

"Karthik, Karthik," a voice calls for me. It's my mom. I hear her voice in snatches, but I ignore her. Above us, flames shoot up, maybe fifty feet high. Where is Juhi and her family? Did they get out? Are there people inside? I keep thinking how the last time I saw Juhi, I wouldn't talk to her, and it's filling me with dread.

I reach the barricades that surround the store on all sides. It's not possible to get any closer. Beyond them are firefighters and the police and several trucks, including two ambulances. There is a great big hose pointed at the fifty-foot flames, and behind the hoses and firefighters there are paramedics and some people on stretchers, though I don't recognize any of their soot-covered faces.

I feel Miles and Binh next to me. Miles is staring at the blaze with a mixture of awe and horror. He keeps pushing up his glasses. "Whoa. Whoa, whoa, whoa."

"We have to find Juhi," I tell them. "Did her family get out?"

"Look!" Binh points to a group of people sitting on the ground. In the center is a tall man, and I recognize him as Satish Shah. I recognize him and I don't. He looks anguished. Someone is treating his face for burns, and his arm is already bandaged. He seems okay, and yet he's beside himself. Next to him are some of the workers from the kitchen, faces I now recognize, too. But where is Juhi?

"It happened in a flash," Satish Shah moans. "I don't understand it. With all the equipment. The sprinklers. I don't understand."

"You will talk to the investigator soon," the paramedic tells him. "Right now, we need to take care of you. Rest."

No one is talking about Juhi. There are just Satish Shah and the workers. Is it possible she wasn't there when the fire happened? Then Binh pulls me over to one of the stretchers. We're still on the other side of the barricade, but we can stand close enough to see who it is.

A police officer approaches us. "Step away," she orders. "This is an active fire. We need everyone to go home. Please."

The person on the stretcher is completely bandaged around

her head, and her face is dark and streaked with soot. But we recognize her immediately. A woman stands next to Juhi's stretcher, and she's crying.

"Juhi!" Binh calls out to her. "Karthik and Binh, we are here."

Meanwhile, I can't find any words. It is too horrible seeing Juhi hurt.

She hears us right away. "Binh? Karthik? What are you doing here?" she calls back, surprised.

The woman next to her looks up, and now I see it's Mrs. Shah. The last time I saw her was at the temple after the dance performance, when she was mad at us for being late.

"Are you okay?" I ask fearfully, finally finding my voice.

Juhi struggles to sit up. "Karthik, I'm . . ."

"Stay down, miss," the person treating her says. He looks at a second technician. "You ready to lift?"

She nods back. "On three."

Together they hoist the stretcher into an ambulance parked behind them.

"You want to ride with us, ma'am?" one of them asks Mrs. Shah.

She nods. She is about to turn when she sees me. "Karthik, is it?" she asks. She squeezes my arm across the barricade and follows the paramedic to the front of the ambulance.

By now my parents are standing next to me, too.

Mom asks one of the paramedics where he's taking Juhi, and he tells them Mass General.

Mom's eyes meet Dad's and he nods.

"Come, Cutie," she says to me. It's the first time in days that she's called me that. "We will take you there."

♪

Mass General is the biggest hospital in Boston, and the busiest. When we get there, it's a snarl of traffic and honking and congested parking. Eventually, we find a parking spot in the visitors' lot, and then we go through a maze of corridors before we get to the emergency room. By then, Juhi has already been sent inside somewhere and we have to sit in the waiting room. Dad and Mom have come with me, and so has Miles. Binh had to stay back because his parents wanted him to help at the restaurant. It had become a staging area for firefighters and police officers, and there had been of flood of people stopping by for water and shelter from the smoke and debris.

In the waiting room, Mom and Dad talk about House of Chaat.

"What will Satish Shah do?" Mom murmurs. "It will take months to recover. If he ever will in this recession."

Dad says, "He will. The insurance will help. And we the community must help him, too. As long as no one is hurt. That's what matters."

"That's Asha Shah's sister who's here, isn't it, Cutie?" Mom asks me.

"Juhi," Dad says. "She comes to the store with her mother. She used to, at least. Don't worry, she will be okay, Karthu, God willing."

I don't know if he's right. Her head was bandaged, and it was hard to tell. I'm still feeling bad for not talking to her before. I'm confused about what's right anymore. But it's nice that my parents have brought me without asking much, like how I'm such good friends with Juhi all of a sudden.

Even Miles came. No one asked him. He just got into the car with us. We called his parents when we got to the hospital. His parents seemed worried, but Miles kept telling them he was okay and he'd get a ride home later.

While my parents talk more about the fire and Satish Shah, I lean over to Miles. "Thanks for coming," I tell him. "You didn't have to."

"Yeah, no problem. We all know how you feel about Juhi Shah."

I give him a look of surprise. "Wait, what do you mean? I'm not—"

"Dude, it's obvious." He's rifling through the sheets of newspaper on the table in front of us. "Friday crossword. Score. Let's do this while we're waiting. You got a pen, Mrs. Raghavan?"

She pulls one out of her handbag. "For you, Mr. Miles, always."

Then she moves over to sit next to him, and we do the crossword while we wait in the emergency room at Mass General.

♪

It takes two hours for me to see Juhi. During that time, Dad calls Nitya and tells her where we are. We all get pizza from the cafeteria. On our way back, we run into the rest of Juhi's family, who had been waiting in another area. They update us on what's happened back at the House of Chaat so far. The fire has been stopped. Everyone got out safely with no major injuries. The only people who got hurt were the ones in the kitchen where the fire started. No one's sure what started it, except that there was a loud clap, when the air above the stoves suddenly ignited.

"Juhi's apron caught on fire," says one of them. Juhi's aunt, I think.

"What?" I exclaim. This is too awful to believe.

"She rolled on the ground," Juhi's aunt explains. "Someone stamped it out with a towel. Quick thinking. She is okay, I hope. Very lucky girl. The restaurant, not so lucky."

"Smoke damage is too much," someone else says. "Poor Satish."

"Where is Satish now?" Dad asks.

"He's inside," Juhi's aunt says. "But I hear he is getting discharged soon. He's okay."

While they talk, I'm still picturing what happened to Juhi when her apron was on fire. She hated that thing. She complained about it all the time. And now it almost killed her.

A few minutes later, Mrs. Shah comes over to us. "Karthik," she says to me. "Juhi wants to see you."

Miles looks at me and pushes up his glasses. My parents watch me, too. Then my mom nudges me. "See how she is, Cutie. Go."

Dad nods. "Tell her we are all wishing her a strong recovery."

I nod at them and follow Mrs. Shah into the corridor.

"She is tired. But she wanted to see you before she sleeps."

"Is she . . . okay?" I don't know how to ask what I really want to ask, which is how badly injured Juhi is, so I can be prepared. The thing is, I don't like hospitals. I don't even like going to the dentist. I hate the smell of alcohol and the sight of blood, and being in a hospital reminds me of all the things about the human body that freak me out. Still, I want to pull it together for Juhi.

"She is very, very lucky," Mrs. Shah says. "You will see for yourself."

We arrive at the room where Juhi is seated in a hospital bed. She's wearing a hospital gown and the blanket is up past her waist, but she's sitting up, eating toast, and *Dawson's Creek* is on the overhead TV. She brightens when she sees me.

"I'm going to check on Satish Bhaiya," Mrs. Shah says to us, and then it's just Juhi and me. I sit on a chair next to the bed.

"I can't believe you came, Karthik," she says.

"Miles is here, too," I say. "He's in the waiting area with my parents."

"You all came? Oh my god, that's so nice." She holds a bandaged hand up to her heart. She reaches to turn down the volume on the TV.

"That's Nitya's favorite show," I say.

"Asha's, too!"

I nod. "So, are you okay?" I look at her bandaged head and arm.

"Yeah," she says. "I have minor burns on my arm and face. They said I won't have any scarring at all on my face. I'm really lucky. Only on my arm, and that's a little bit, from when my hair caught on fire."

"Your hair? God."

"Yeah, freaky, isn't it? That was the scariest part. I could smell my hair burning. And hear it. The sizzling sound. I don't think I'll ever forget that." Juhi's voice wavers momentarily. "But as soon as it happened, this guy, Rahul, threw a towel over my head. He snuffed it out. Like in an instant."

"Wow."

"Righto," she says.

I smile unconsciously. I haven't heard that word in a long time.

"So you're okay," I say. "That's good."

"It's majorly good. Only . . ." Juhi's voice trails off. "I don't know what will happen to my uncle's restaurant. My dad still has his 7-Eleven. But I'm not sure what Satish Uncle will do."

"There's insurance."

"Yeah, but will it be enough? And will it pay for the time he loses?" She looks down at the hospital sheet, tracing a pattern with a finger from her nonbandaged hand. "Karthik, I'm glad you came. I never expected to see you at the restaurant. You know, when it was burning."

"Binh came and got me."

"Right. He's nice. You're all so nice." She pauses, looking up at the TV, and I can see the lights from the screen reflected in her eyes. "Karthik, also I want to say I'm sorry."

"For what?" I catch my breath. I don't know why I ask when I think I already know.

Juhi frowns hard, and it takes me a moment to realize she's making this face so she won't cry. "I'm not proud of myself for missing your dress rehearsal," she says, still looking at the TV. "I know it was important. I don't know why I do the things I do. I can't even explain it to myself. But I should have been there that day." She looks at me finally. "I want you to know that."

"It's fine," I say awkwardly. "Don't worry about it." I try to brush it off. She still looks like she wants to cry, and I don't want her to do that. But also I don't want her to be nice to me all of a sudden. There is something worse about that. I've already decided I don't want to let her into my life too much. I know I'll only get hurt. A fire isn't going to change that. I get up from the chair.

"Wait, Karthik. Don't go," Juhi pleads. "I thought you might understand because you're Indian, too. That it's hard to be different from everyone else."

Her eyes are swollen from the fire, and there is a bruise along her brow. But with the bandage around her head, her hair is pulled back and she looks younger, almost like she did in third grade. And I notice that her eyes are the same. The same size and shape and depth. I read somewhere that we're born with the eyes we're going to have for the rest of our life. They don't get bigger, we just grow into them. Maybe that's why there are so many songs written about eyes. Even Maria, when she's singing about Tony, she says in her eyes there's only him. Because the eyes are the truth. They are the thing that stays the same when the rest of us changes.

"I guess I think it's harder," I say slowly, "being the same as everyone else."

She looks surprised. "I never thought of it that way."

"You don't have to be like everybody, Juhi."

"You're right," she says unsurely.

We look at each other. There is a silence. I think it's strange how even now she doesn't mention Jacob by name. Is it that she can't, or she won't?

I rock on my feet. I stuff my hands in my pockets. It seems like she's waiting for me to say or do something. I could leave. I could say, later. Isn't that what other people would do?

But somehow that doesn't feel right. And it's not because there was a fire. Because maybe I'm not cool like Jacob or Hoodie. But what if I choose to be the nice guy every time? What's wrong with that?

I reach for the remote. "*Dawson's Creek* is all right," I tell her, "but let's watch something else."

"*Star Trek*!" she exclaims when I find the station. She howls and gives me grief about Mr. Spock, and I tell her the new seasons are so much better. And we keep watching. We make fun of everything—the ads, the script, the way the starship *Enterprise* looks like a plastic toy you'd find in a cereal box, but then she says the show is actually better than she'd thought. And just like that, it's okay. Even with us being in a hospital room. So much has happened to us both and to our families. Yet here we are, and somehow it's all good between Juhi and me.

Chapter 39

The restaurant is a different story.

The fire at House of Chaat burned for approximately an hour. The temperature inside got as hot as 2,500 degrees. It melted all the kitchen appliances, destroyed the floor all the way to the counter, and made a hole in the roof. Then the smoke damaged the rest of the restaurant. It was an unmitigated disaster, but one in which no one lost their lives. Everyone said it was a miracle, because it happened at five thirty in the evening, when the dinner crowd was lining up. The cause was clogged grease traps over the stove where oil was heated for frying.

Satish Shah couldn't think straight for days. Maybe it was the smoke inhalation. Or seeing the fire blaze over his head fifty feet in the air. He wouldn't talk to anyone, he didn't go anywhere, he didn't even open the door when my dad went to visit him. Then after the third day, Satish Shah shook himself out of it. He made a bunch of phone calls. He stopped by the grocery store. He didn't say anything to my mom and me at the counter except hi, then he went straight to the back room, where he and my dad spoke for an hour behind the closed door.

When they come out afterward, they're smiling, and Satish Shah claps Dad on the back and calls him a great man.

"Beta, we are missing your deliveries!" he says to me on the way out. "But we move on!"

And then he's gone.

"What," Mom asks, "was that all about?"

"Oh, him," Dad says. "Goes to show you, the universe operates in strange ways. One day he's on top and I'm on bottom. Then he's on bottom and I'm . . . getting a knock on my door."

"What did he want?" Mom is curious. So am I.

Dad sits on a stool. "Well, Satish has a proposal for me. The most fantastic one I've heard. He says House of Chaat was booming until the fire came. And my store was booming until his store came."

Mom is surprised. "He said that? Who says that?"

"Satish Shah," I say. I'm not surprised.

"But now he's out of a store," Dad says. "And so am I. Only not yet."

"Oh?" Mom is trying to understand.

"That's where his proposal comes in," Dad says. "He wants to know, what if he and I join forces? What if instead of rebuilding House of Chaat where it is, he rebuilds it next door in Mr. Miller's old deli? And I stay on and we go into business together? We sell chaat *and* groceries. We sell food ready to eat and food ready to cook and everything in between. That way, the groceries continue, the deliveries continue, the chaat continues, but now we face this recession together. Like brothers."

Mom is dumbstruck.

So am I. What is Dad talking about? Join forces with Juhi's family? In *West Side Story*, Tony kills Maria's brother, Bernardo, in a gang fight. Then Chino, Bernardo's right-hand man, kills Tony. Maria's family and Tony's family are enemies. And nothing gets better between them until Tony dies.

But in my life, Dad says our families could be joining together. Could this be a way out for everyone?

Mom finally finds her voice. "That's wonderful, Manjesh. You could keep the store. Isn't that what you want? And hopefully, you will stay afloat, not lose money, and . . ." Her voice trails off.

I look at her and I see it in her face. This is not Tony and Bernardo working together. Mom is feeling something else . . . not happiness, but more like her heart is broken. But why?

"Roopa," Dad says. "Roopa."

"It's what you want, isn't it?" Mom says, her voice breaking at the end.

"Do you know what I told him?" he asks. "I said, Satish, you are a good businessman, but you see, my wife and me, we made a decision already. That I work at a job which is steady so she can study and go back to school. It's important I do what I do so she can do what she has to do. Because she did that for me, and now it's my turn. Which is why I cannot work in the store anymore."

Mom looks at him in quiet amazement. "You told him that?" she asks.

"Yes," Dad says. "I remembered Karthu's idea."

"But I can't let you do that. You have a chance to bring back the store. And now you're giving it up for me. You'll be miserable, and . . ."

"I won't be," Dad says. "We've talked about this already. I know what I'm doing. I really think this is the right decision. Not just for you, but for the kids and me."

"You'll be in an office," Mom says softly. Her hands sweep around her. "Not here."

Dad smiles at her. "I know where I'll be, Roopa."

Mom takes a long, shaky breath. Her palm rests on the counter. In my entire life, I have never seen her cry. I stare, transfixed. Is she going to do it now? Am I going to see the waterworks?

Mom breathes in and out. She looks at us both and gives a tremendous smile.

"Come, Cutie," she says. "Help me pack the deliveries."

For a while, Mom and I just pack. There are so many bags because of all the sale items. And now the House of Chaat customers have nowhere else to buy their lunch, so they're coming to us.

"So you're not mad anymore?" I ask.

My mom sets down her clipboard. "Mad? Why would I be mad?"

"You've been mad ever since you found out about Shanthi's play."

"Oh, that," she says. "Okay, so I was. Fine."

"And now you're not?"

"Why didn't you tell me, Cutie? I support the arts. I'm not . . . what do they say? A putz."

"You would be okay with me being in a play? How about during the school year? You would be okay with me spending hours a week at rehearsals?"

"Sure. That Leonard Bernstein went to Harvard, didn't he? But you have to do it the right way. You have to audition, get coaching. It will look real nice on your college application."

"No. I don't want to do that."

"Do what?"

"I don't want to do it to get into college."

Mom stands back. "Why not? If you do it the right way . . ."

"Because I need to know if I really do like it first." I try to think of a way to make her understand. "It's like ordering Polly Wants Pistachio when you've been ordering Caramel Swirl all your life."

"What are you talking about?"

"How will I know I like pistachio ice cream until I try it?"

Mom looks at me, exasperated. "Life is very hard, Cutie. You don't always get to like everything. You don't always have time to figure out if you like Polly Pistachio or not."

"If I don't have time to find out when I'm young, when will I?"

Outside, a police siren goes off and it reminds me of the fire. I see Mom looking out the window, and I wonder if she's thinking the same thing.

"I guess I could ease up," she says. "God only knows, life is short. You never know what's going to happen. One day your store is there, the next day it's gone. But time is so precious, Cutie, you don't always get a second chance to do things."

"You did."

Mom flushes. She fingers a pen resting on the counter. "So how are you going to figure this thing out? If you like acting?"

"I've thought about that, actually." It feels good to say these words out loud when I've only been rehearsing them in my head. "I want to try out for the school play. And I want to learn by watching plays in a real theater. Like the Boston Opera House."

"But that's so expensive, Cutie. Do you have any idea how much those tickets cost?"

"They have student discounts. Plus, I'm going to tutor a kid who lives across from Mrs. Rodrigues, one of our customers. He's in fifth grade and needs help in school. They're going to pay me ten dollars an hour."

"You're going to work so you can see plays?"

"Leonard Bernstein paid for his piano lessons by teaching other kids."

Mom doesn't say anything for a moment, but I can see her looking at me with new respect. "Huh. I guess it's better than working for free at the store."

I nod. "That's what I thought."

Dad calls from the back room. "Roopa, come help me. Something's not adding up here."

Just then, the front door of the store opens.

Mom points to me as she goes back. "Help that customer. And okay, Cutie. Maybe you have something here. Learning by working. I like that. But don't get so cocky about it."

Cocky about it? Only my mom would say something like that.

A woman with salt-and-pepper hair approaches the counter. She is wearing an Indian print top and slacks, and on her arm she carries a leather handbag.

"Hello," she says, smiling. "You are much younger than I remember you."

I look at her, puzzled. I don't remember this woman at all, and I have a good memory.

"Just kidding. I think it's your father I saw here many years ago." Her voice is deep and musical, with only a hint of an Indian accent. And now she does seem familiar, but I can't say how.

"Do you want me to get my dad?"

She waves her hand. "No need. I'll just have a look around, thank you."

The woman stays for a while, walking slowly through the aisles. Eventually she comes to the front with her basket filled. It's mostly vegetables and spices, and a bag of spicy hot chips.

"My daughter loves these," she says when I ring her up and get to the chips. "You're the only store that's carried them all these years."

When she says that, it dawns on me why this woman looks so familiar.

"Do you want to buy more for her? Um, since we're closing."

As usual, I don't know what I'm doing. With Mrs. Rodrigues and Mr. Jain, it was easy to help them because they wanted to be helped. With my mom, I had to try a couple of times before she started to listen. But this woman, I'm not even sure if she is who I think she is.

Then I look at her credit card and I get my answer. Deepti Ananth. Shanthi's mom, in the flesh.

Meanwhile, she shakes her head. "She doesn't come by these days. But that's another story."

I pack her groceries, taking care not to squash the produce at the bottom. "You could ask her over, and say you have the spicy hot chips. That might work."

Mrs. Ananth's eyes fill. "It's like you know my daughter," she says.

"Maybe I do," I say.

I remember the flyer my mom brought back the other day. I find it on the counter under a stack of papers.

"Here." I hand the flyer to Mrs. Ananth. "You can see what she's been up to."

Chapter 40

We decide to meet at Carmine's one last time.

"I can't believe you'll be in Weymouth tomorrow," I say. "Who lives *way* out in Weymouth?"

"Which *way* is Weymouth?" Binh asks.

We're sitting around a booth. Binh and I have been teasing Miles all afternoon about the "way" in Weymouth. We're joking, but the truth is that I'm really sad Miles is leaving. I can't imagine what school will be like without him.

"Weymouth is a *waste* of time," Miles says as he eats his usual Sloopy-Goopy on a cone.

"Waste of time. That's a good one," Binh says. He and I ordered the same ice cream, New England Cookie Dough, in a bowl. It's melting fast, but at least it's in a bowl.

The door opens and it's Juhi and Sara. My jaw drops when I see them. I had emailed Juhi this morning that it was Miles's last day and she should come to Carmine's. But that's not why I'm surprised as they walk over to our booth.

"You cut your hair," Binh says.

Juhi's hair is still super straight, but now it comes up to her ears. It's shorter than mine.

"Why?" I ask, still surprised.

She sits next to me as Binh makes room for Sara on the other side.

"After the fire, my hair smelled like smoke. Everyone told me they couldn't smell it, but I could," Juhi says. "Plus, I just wanted a change. Something different."

"I like it," Sara says. "Makes your neck look long."

"Yeah. Like I'm a giraffe," Juhi says.

"You're a giraffe," Sara says.

Why is Sara even here? I wonder. I'm still trying to get used to Juhi's haircut. She looks like a completely different person. Everything is different except her eyes. Her eyes are the same.

"I have news," Binh says.

"About your new school?" Miles says.

"Kind of. The news is that I'm not going to it," Binh says.

We all murmur questions at him. Why not? What happened?

"We were all set with me going. All of us. Me as well," Binh explains. "Then the fire happens. My parents see that. They don't like it. We are all afraid of the bad luck and the uncertain times. It is important for us to save. To wait and see. Also more important. I like Allston. I like my friends. I want to be here with all of you."

He looks at Miles and me and then his eyes rest on Sara. Her face is red, but they keep looking at each other and smile shyly. Oh my god. They like each other! Binh likes Sara. Stick-up-her-butt Sara! Does Miles know? When I look at him, he just rolls his eyes. Of course. I'm always the last one to figure out these things.

I guess we're all so busy talking that I don't even hear Jacob and Hoodie come in until they're standing at the booth in front of us.

Juhi says, "Hi, Jacob, hi, Hoodie."

Jacob looks at her hair curiously. "Did the fire do that?" he asks.

Everyone laughs. Maybe because it's the stupidest thing anyone could say.

"No," Juhi says. "Of course not."

"It's short," Hoodie says. "You look like a boy."

"So what?" I tell him.

"Kar-dick," Jacob announces breezily.

"Kar-dick," Hoodie repeats. He's been holding a basketball under his arm and now he starts bouncing it. Once. Twice.

"We need some new jokes," Jacob says. "Juhi didn't find them funny last time."

"What jokes, the ones about Kar-dick?" Hoodie asks.

"Yeah, those. She didn't like the one about the car breaking."

Hoodie snickers.

The whole time, Binh is glaring. Miles is pushing up his glasses uncomfortably. And Sara looks torn between her loyalty to Binh and staying on Jacob's good side.

"Juhi, you wanted a new Kar-dick joke, right?" Jacob asks her.

Juhi, who's been eating her Dark Cherry cone from the bottom like she always does, stops chewing.

"It's Karthik," I say.

"What?" Jacob asks.

"It's Karthik." My voice rises. "You're saying my name wrong."

Jacob holds his hands up. "Maybe your name is hard to say."

"Yeah, your name is hard to say," says Hoodie. *Bounce, bounce.*

"So get it right," I say evenly. "Or we'll get your name wrong."

"Yeah, like what if," Juhi says suddenly, "we call you Jackass?"

For a moment, everyone's speechless. Even Jacob doesn't know what to say.

Then we laugh. And the weird thing is, Jacob laughs, too. He gets a sheepish look but he smiles along, and he takes off his baseball cap and puts it back on.

"All right, my bad. Smell you later, Kar-*thik*."

"See you later, Jackass," I say. "I mean, Jacob."

More laughter. But the good kind. The kind where I'm not the one being laughed at.

Then he and Hoodie leave. They don't even buy ice cream; they just saunter off through the door and down the street.

"Let's keep calling him Jackass," Sara says.

Of course she would. She's such an instigator.

"Nah," I say. "He got the hint."

"I wouldn't mind calling him Jackass," Miles says. "But I'm moving."

Everyone keeps talking and joking while I eat my New England Cookie Dough slowly out of my bowl, savoring the taste of sweet and salt in my mouth. It's just like this summer. A mix of everything.

When I'm done with my ice cream, I sneak a look at Juhi. I'm still not used to her hair, to seeing the line of her jaw and length of her neck. She catches me watching her. And I'm not sure who does it first, but under the table her fingers brush mine. And then I reach out for the first time, and I hold Juhi's hand.

♪

Okay, so I held Juhi's hand! The whole time we sat in the booth at Carmine's. We acted casual, nobody said anything about it, not even us. We didn't look at each other, while under the table her hand felt warm in mine. I want to say that after holding Juhi's hand, I'm all set. I know how it's going to be between us. But I don't. I still don't know anything. I don't know anything when we leave Carmine's or when I get home, about whether I should email her, or call her, or do nothing . . . or something. It's a completely new world ahead of me. But for now, she's in it.

A LIST ABOUT LISTS IN 3 PARTS

- I might still use them.
- They're good for ice cream flavors.
- Not people.

Because people are more than lists, they're the spaces between words, the things I don't know yet about them, the way they change and will keep changing.

♪

It's the night of the performance. I'm backstage in the BU theater and the seats are filling up as I peek from behind the curtains. The audience is peppered with people I know. Mrs. Rodrigues has come with Mr. Rodrigues and the older Mrs. Rodrigues. They're seated in the front. Mr. Jain is in the back with a Styrofoam cup in his hand, most likely his chai. Near him are Binh, Sara, Juhi, and Miles, who is back from Weymouth to see the performance. Three rows from them is my family. My mom has brought flowers. I'm afraid she will embarrass me by giving them to me in front of everyone, but mostly I'm glad she came. She's already pulled her first all-nighter studying for a quiz, so maybe that has taken the mom-edge off her. Meanwhile, Dad is taking pictures and Nitya is craning her neck to see who else has come.

Five other plays are being performed this evening, too, and all of them are listed in the program. I've read through the actor bios and everyone has a long list of acting credits and degrees. Next to my name it reads: *high school freshman residing in Allston.* Shanthi tells me that being the youngest is the best credit of all.

So far, high school is a breeze. Most days, I don't see Mom in the mornings, because she has to leave early for her chem class. Dad has been gone early, too, for a training session at his new job. The store is empty, with nothing left except for a few crates. Nitya walks to the high school with her friends and tells me not to talk to her unless I need help. Otherwise I should stick to my "fresh people." Every day, Binh meets me at the corner of Comm Ave and we walk together. Sometimes before the bell rings, we hang out by the front doors with

Juhi and Sara, who's now surprisingly nice and says my name right. There are already posters up for the high school musical: *Singin' in the Rain*. Auditions are in a month. I'm practicing the songs. I've seen the video of Gene Kelly getting drenched in the rain and dancing with his umbrella as he sings. I think I could do that, too. I've also started tutoring Harry, the boy next door to the Rodrigueses. After I help him with his homework, Mrs. R makes me come over for mango lassi. I guess some things don't change. I've already saved up forty dollars. By next month, I can buy my first play ticket. I'm thinking of seeing *Cats*. Shanthi says she will come with me. I don't tell her that she reminded me of one when I first met her.

In the theater, the lights are starting to dim. There's a hush backstage as the five different casts get ready. Shanthi fixes my hair with gel and straightens my collar.

It's on the tip of my tongue to tell her I invited her mom to the play. When I looked out earlier, I couldn't tell if Mrs. Ananth was there. I guess I'll let Shanthi find out for herself. Maybe she will spot her mom in the crowd and her heart will melt, and she won't have to carry the burden of her art alone. And I'll be like Aunt Clara, only I'm not sending a piano. I'm sending her mom.

"You look great," Shanthi whispers to me. "How do you feel?"

"Like barfing," I say.

"Good. It means you're ready." She looks me over one last time. "You're the brother I never had, you know that?" Her cat eyes are a little teary as she says this.

"You're like a sister," I say, "and I have one of those."

She hands me a small box. "I told you I'd get you something."

I'm conscious of everyone sitting outside, waiting for us, but I open it, wondering what on earth it could be. Nestled inside the box are two gold buttons. Cuff links.

"Go ahead," she says. "Kiss them."

"Oh man, thanks!" I'm surprised she remembered, though not surprised at all. I do as she says, kissing the cuff links awkwardly. "I guess I have to buy a dress shirt now," I say.

When Shanthi steps out onstage to introduce her play, the butterflies start up in my stomach. In a few moments, the audience will be looking at me. I imagine them, my family and friends and Juhi, all recognizing me, but wondering for the first time who I might be.

I imagine another person, too. He's ten years old and banging his fingers, he's twenty-five with a fearless baton, he's an old man who laughs easily. His hands are immense, he's playing the piano, he's playing all the music in the world. Lenny whispers in my ear, *Something's coming*. My feet reach the stage and I whisper, "*It's here.*"

Author's Note

Every generation experiences at least one event that tests and shapes them, whether it's a war, an economic recession, or a health crisis. During the financial crisis of 2008–09, the United States banking system crashed, sending shock waves through the world as families in America were suddenly without homes, retirement savings, or jobs.

Yet some of our best artists, writers, and musicians arise from our darkest moments. Leonard Bernstein grew up during the Great Depression, the son of Russian Jewish immigrants, and he became one of the most beloved and famous musicians in America. Not only was he known for many legendary musicals, including *West Side Story*, but he was also a gifted pianist, conductor, and teacher.

In many ways, Lenny embodies the American Dream: Work hard and you can do anything. Lenny rose to the greatest heights through sheer determination, talent, and good will. That Lenny should be Karthik's inspiration seems obvious. Lenny would have turned one hundred years old in 2018, ten years after the financial crisis hit America.

Karthik comes to realize by the end of the book that success isn't an all-or-nothing game. His mom supposes that Lenny Bernstein had "the genes" for music. But being successful is so much more than your DNA or how hard you work in school. It's about giving yourself the time to try new things and allowing yourself the privilege of doing them badly before doing them well.

I'm sure that Lenny would agree.

Acknowledgments

I've always loved Indian grocery stores, ever since I was in grad school and took the T from Allston to Brookline to shop at one for the first time. I didn't cook much then (I was famous for making a lot of rasam), but those first trips left a lasting impression on me. Like Karthik's dad, I think Indian grocery stores are a meeting ground to see others who cook the same foods as me and to find those ingredients that remind me of home. In the 1970s, when my family and I first arrived in Iowa from Bangalore, India, the nearest Indian grocery store was in Chicago, a four-hour drive away. Today, there's a store only minutes from my house. I'm grateful for all of that: the four-hour journeys, the T-ride to Brookline, and the ten-minute drive to my local store. I want to acknowledge the sweetness of being able to cook some of the same dishes I remember eating as a child both here and in India.

Mostly, it's my kids who play instruments these days, but I'm so happy that growing up, I got to play the violin, especially as a member of the Washington-Idaho Symphony, with whom I performed music from Leonard Bernstein's *West Side Story*. How fortunate I was to encounter the genius of that musical, whose rhythms, melodies, and soul have been with me ever since. Even today, hearing "One Hand, One Heart" will bring tiny, private tears to my eyes.

It took me twelve years to write, rewrite, and reenvision this story in front of you—an amalgamation of time spent in different cities and different grocery stores and of being a violinist and learning to write.

For the making of this story, I'm grateful to Steven Malk, my incredible agent who has seen this book from its early days and who had the grace and smarts to tell me when it wasn't ready and then, at last, when it finally was. Thank you, Steve, for seeing me through all these drafts, for not giving up, and for being the one to send this work out into the world.

Thank you to Erica Finkel, my talented editor who loved *Karthik Delivers* as soon as she read it and who has worked with me to bring Karthik to life both on the cover and inside these pages. Thank you to the entire team at Abrams who have helped me make this a better book and share it with the rest of the world. Thank you to Katelan Thomas—your cover art turned Karthik into a real person!

My deepest gratitude to my writing partners, Sayantani DasGupta, Veera Hiranandani, and Heather Tomlinson, who read so many drafts (and I'm talking so many). When you work on a novel for twelve years, often there is a voice inside you asking, *Why on earth is it taking you so long??* My sweet writing partners helped me push that voice away.

Thank you to my parents and my brother (how else would I know about sibling humor?), and to my dearest Suresh, Keerthana, and Meera, for eating everything I cook (except eggplant). No writing life would ever be complete or worth it without all of you. Love always.

About the Author

Sheela Chari is the author of the Unexplainable Disappearance of Mars Patel series, based on the Peabody Award–winning mystery podcast; *Finding Mighty*, a Junior Library Guild Selection and Children's Choice Award finalist; and *Vanished*, an APALA Children's Literature Honor Book, Edgar finalist, and Al's Book Club pick on the *Today Show*. Sheela has degrees from Stanford University, Boston University, and New York University, where she received an MFA in fiction. She is a faculty member in the Writing for Children and Young Adults MFA program at the Vermont College of Fine Arts. She lives with her family in New York.